Other Books by: P. Lee May

For Children:

Laurie's Secret

For Parents and Teenagers:

Protecting Your Child in Prayer

You're Gonna Make It! A Christian guide of wisdom keys for single parents

For Everyone:

Taking Authority Over Your Neighborhood

Since Jesus Came to My House

Friends

Share

Secrets

God's Heartbeat, LLC
Published in USA

This work is entirely fictional. Any similarity, to actual people living or dead, events, or locales, is entirely coincidental. The names, places, characters, situations, and incidents are products of the author's imagination and revelation used fictionally and inspirationally.

Most scriptures used are from the *King James Bible* (KJV) unless otherwise stated. Other scripture references are from the New International Version Bible (NIV) and the New Living Translation Bible (NLT).

Library of Congress Control Number: 2015916347 for (hardcopy: paperback)
ISBN: 978-0-9846410-8-6 (hardcopy: paperback),
ISBN: 978-0-9846410-9-3 (eBook)

Author: P. Lee May

Published by:
God's Heartbeat, LLC
16011 S. Kedzie Ave. #536
Markham, IL 60428,
Email: godsheartbeat_inc@yahoo.com

This book is dedicated to my Lord and savior:
Jesus Christ, Father God and Holy Ghost;
my daughters: Jameta, Presita, Dolorita, and Juliet;
my grandchildren: Brandon, Jeremiah, Jerry III (Tre R.I.P.), Josiah, Jerred, Makay'a, and Paige;
and my friends: Rev. Anne V. Johnson and Barbara Ost.

Table of Contents

Chapter 1
Julie's Friend - Wendy

Giggling, Julie and Wendy sit side-by-side on Wendy's front porch. They just arrived home from school at 3:30 p.m. Wendy's mum let them go outside for one hour before they have to do their homework. Normally, Julie went home to her white and blue ranch house two streets west of Wendy's beige brick bungalow. But the two 12-year-old best friends had arranged with their parents the previous week to spend this afternoon together.

"You know, Wen," Julie starts. "I think my new favorite color is lime green. It's the bomb color! I'm gonna ask Mama to take me to the Silver Valley Mall so that I can find something lime green to go with the shirt I got last week. I'll ask if you can go with us, okay?"

"Your favorite color changes all the time!" Wendy teases. She flips her long coal black hair out of her freckled face with her right hand.

"Last week it was purple, because your mama's favorite color is purple just like me. Last month it was pink because your cousin, JoJo, likes pink and the month before that it was orange. Two weeks ago, it was red again because your favorite stuffed animals always wear something red. Remember, that's the reason you have so much red in your closet now and why you changed into those red jean shortalls after school today," Wendy says, looking Julie directly in the eye. Wendy places a hand on an imaginary large hip. "Imaginary hips" are what Julie's mama says both she and Julie have.

Giggling again, Julie shifts her body and stretches out her thin, chocolate legs.

"I know I change colors a lot. And I have to admit I'll always like red because my favorite stuffed animals usually wear something with red in it. Red has always been my **first** favorite color. But you know a girl's got to expand her wardrobe. And what better way to do it than to add more cool colors?" Julie says as she hi-fives Wendy.

"And you know it! I need some more colors in my closet, myself!" Wendy says.

As the girls laugh, Wendy stretches out her long freckled legs. Calling to her mum, Wendy asks if they may take a walk to the park before they start their homework. They have only been on the porch for 15 minutes and Wendy knows if she wants to talk privately with Julie, she needs to be away from her house because her mum has the window opened and is trying to listen to every word they say.

"Wen, do you have on your watch?" Wendy's mum yells.

"Yes, Mum. I do," Wendy calls back.

"Well, I'll expect you two back in 45 minutes," Wendy's mum says.

Moving quickly, the two girls start walking before Wendy's mum changes her mind. Straightening out her vibrant purple, knee-length shortalls, Wendy pats Julie on the head. Wendy is over four inches taller than Julie is, although there is only a week difference in their ages. They were both born in August of 1987, when it was hot outside. Wendy's mum and Julie's mama always say the same thing, "I sweated buckets when I was pregnant with you!" Both mothers said they don't ever want to have a baby due in August again. And so far, Wendy and Julie are each their last child born.

When they were about a block away, Wendy feels that they are far enough away to discuss what's on her mind.

"Julie, we're best friends for life, aren't we?" Wendy asks as she slows her pace.

"And you know it, girl! Why do you ask?" Julie replies.

"Well, if we're best friends, then promise me when we get old and become old foggy adults, like our parents, we'll still be best friends even if we go to different high schools and colleges and live in different cities!" Wendy says.

"Girl, of course, we're gonna be best friends. We've been best friends since our mothers met when we were 3 years old. You think you're gonna get rid of me that easily?" Julie replies as she stops walking to look Wendy in the face.

"What's wrong with you anyway?" Julie inquires. When Wendy hesitates to answer, Julie continues.

"Don't we tell each other everything? Well, almost everything, 'cause I don't want to know when you get your period? And how many times you have to do number two in the bathroom!" Julie says.

"I know that's right! Me neither!" Wendy says. Turning the corner, they walk east from where Wendy lives. At the end of the block, they cross the street.

"It's just that Mum used to have a black girl friend, Jasmine, as her best friend from the time she was 5 years old until she was 12..." Wendy says.

Julie interrupts and asks,

"Since when do you qualify as only being a white girl? Did you forget about your daddy?" Julie asks.

"You know what I mean. I know we both are mixed. But let me finish the rest of the story," Wendy says. Julie's mama is black and her dad is Hispanic, while Wendy's mum is white from England and her father is Indian from India. Wendy's dad's genes are where Wendy gets her coal black hair.

"Mum and Jasmine used to have so much fun together just like you and me. They went to the same church together. They had sleepovers at Mum's house because Jasmine had six brothers and sisters in their three-bedroom house. Mum only had Uncle Bud and Auntie Geri in their three-bedroom apartment," Wendy says.

"Mum and Jasmine used to walk home from school together to Mum's apartment building. The sleepovers stopped one day when Mum and Jasmine were about 12 years old. Mum didn't see Jasmine in school for over a week during that time. For a long time, Jasmine couldn't talk to Mum on the telephone and she never came over to Mum's house again. As a matter of fact, Mum couldn't understand why?" Wendy says.

"Things changed a lot after that. Mum's family moved on the other side of town. Mum and Jasmine went to two different high schools. Mum and Jasmine tried to keep in touch but it didn't always work out. After they graduated from high school, they went to two different colleges and wrote letters to each other. Mum invited Jasmine to be in her wedding and Jasmine invited Mum to be in her wedding. But they didn't have the same closeness they used to have," Wendy says.

"Before you get started again, I just want to say, something terrible must have happened to Jasmine. Did your mum and Jasmine tell each other almost everything like we do?" Julie asks.

"Mum says they did up until that one day. If I tell you,

you've got to promise me you will not, I mean will not tell anybody! **Nooo body you hear**! Mum, don't even realize I heard everything," Wendy says. Wendy's eyes widened.

"You know I can keep a secret. I didn't tell anybody how you laughed so hard you couldn't make it to the bathroom and peed on yourself when we were watching *Jungle 2 Jungle* two years ago!" Julie says, blinking her eyes rapidly as if she has been insulted.

"Okay, so you can keep a secret. My auntie Geri is 5 years older and my uncle Bud is 3 years older than Mum is. This is what happened. Auntie Geri was awake when the police came to Mum's apartment real late that night: the night Jasmine was supposed to come over after school.

"It seems my uncle Bud told his friends how fine Jasmine was 'cause she had real hips! Not imaginary ones like us. And she had boobs! Mum said Jasmine jumped from wearing a training bra to wearing a 'C' cup right away when she was 11 years old. So by the time Jasmine was 12, she was wearing a 'DD' cup!" Wendy says as she holds her hands extended in front of her own breasts.

"Dang! And we only wear 'AA' cups! She was big!" Julie says pushing her chest forward to imagine what a "DD" would look like on her. The girls stop inside McGarrett Park and sit down on a bench.

"I listened from the outside of the dining room while Mum talked to Auntie Geri five nights ago. And I waited on the stairs when Mum told Father, later that same night. I was supposed to be working on my report. Auntie Geri finally told Mum what happened to Jasmine that week in December around Christmas, when they were 12 years old and the reason why Jasmine couldn't spend the night at

Mum's house anymore," Wendy says as she looks around to make sure no one is near them by the park bench.

"Anyway, Jasmine had gotten permission to spend the night at Mum's house and Mum didn't know it. It was supposed to be a surprise to Mum because Jasmine's parents were gonna let Jasmine stay the whole week. She was so excited that Jasmine ran over to Mum's apartment building to surprise Mum with the news and didn't wait for any of her brothers or sisters to walk her over. Jasmine told them she would be fine by herself. With so many brothers and sisters, she wanted alone time to plan things in her mind for the week without listening to them," Wendy says.

Wendy continues telling the story about how Jasmine arrived as Uncle Bud and three of his friends were leaving to go play basketball at the park. They saw Jasmine coming. They decided to see for themselves exactly what Jasmine's boobs looked like because Uncle Bud had told his friends how her boobs bounced when Jasmine walked. As Jasmine entered the building, one of them put his hand over her mouth as another one grabbed both of her arms and tried to pin her arms behind her. Jasmine didn't have six brothers and sisters for nothing. She kicked one boy right between his legs with her army combat boots. He bent over holding himself in the front and let out some curse words.

Wendy continues recalling how Uncle Bud's other friend let go of Jasmine's mouth because she bit him on his hand. But another friend said,

"It's four of us against her, come on y'all! We can do this. We just want to see the girl's boobs!"

As vividly as possible, Wendy recollects how her uncle Bud, who was the biggest, stepped forward and picked up

Jasmine off the floor. By now, Jasmine was screaming, kicking, punching wildly and crying. Two guys grabbed her legs and the boy, who got kicked between his legs, grabbed an arm and began to pull off her coat. Uncle Bud wrapped Jasmine's scarf around her mouth to keep Jasmine from biting anybody else and held her arm as his friend took Jasmine's other arm out of her coat. They were determined to take Jasmine's bra off.

Julie shakes her head and she interrupts the story saying,

"No, he didn't? Your uncle Bud? The one married to your auntie Betty with three girls? Girl, your first cousins' father! **Your mum's brother, uncle Bud?"** Julie asks.

"Uh, huh! That Uncle Bud. I couldn't believe it myself," Wendy says, softly nodding her head up and down.

"Disgusting! See! That's nasty! Did they see her boobs? Did they rape her?" Julie asks quickly. With all the movies on television, Julie had picked up the word "rape" and wasn't exactly sure what it meant since Mama always turned the station if she thought a rape was about to happen. Julie must have used the right word because Wendy answered right away.

"No, they didn't get a chance to, thank God! You see, Mum's family lived on the third floor and this old lady lived on the first floor," Wendy says as she continues the story.

Wendy repeats her mother's story of how scared the old lady on the first floor was of the teenage boys. Wendy explains how she heard in other stories from Mum about how that old lady always complained to the landlord that Uncle Bud and his friends were up to no good. Well, this time she was right! The old lady heard the scuffle then called the police and the landlord. The old lady was looking through the peephole of her door. The old lady watched as Uncle Bud and his friends attacked Jasmine, who was screaming then silenced.

In the meantime the man and his wife, who lived on the second floor, came in the building. They startled the teenagers. Uncle Bud dropped Jasmine just as the teenagers were getting ready to pull her sweater up above her boobs. All those teenage boys ran out of the hallway as Jasmine fell into the arms of the man's wife shaking and crying. The old lady opened her door and right then both the landlord and the police ran up the walkway. Wendy's mum wasn't sure what that old lady told the police because they were there in a few minutes.

Wendy's mum explained that Auntie Geri heard the whole story when the police came late that night to talk with Wendy's granddad and grandmother; after the police had spoken with all the other boys individually and their parents. Wendy's mum being the youngest was already asleep. Wendy's granddad and grandmother decided to relocate in order to separate Uncle Bud from his friends.

Later, they had to go to court. Uncle Bud and his friends were under court supervision for one year. The next year, Auntie Geri stayed with friends in the old neighborhood to finish out her senior year in high school after Wendy's mum graduated from eighth grade. Because Uncle Bud was the reason for the move, he was out of luck. He transferred to the new high school right away as soon as the family moved.

Auntie Geri said Mum was never told because she and Jasmine were such good friends and the family didn't want to upset Mum. Mum's family only told her that my granddad had a change in his job so they had to move.

Wendy comments that when Auntie Geri finished telling her mum what happened all those years ago, Wendy's mum cried for a long time. Afterwards, Mum told Father what she and Auntie Geri discussed.

Wendy tells Julie that Wendy's mum called Jasmine the next day to ask Jasmine, why she never talked to her about it? Mum found out Jasmine did not say anything to Mum because Jasmine was so ashamed and embarrassed. As Wendy continues the story, she explains that Jasmine thought Wendy's mum knew already.

Jasmine's father never let her forget how she almost got raped and how if her brothers and sisters had walked her to Mum's apartment, nothing would have ever happened. Wendy's mum and Jasmine cried together for over 20 minutes on the telephone. Wendy's mum apologized for her family, especially Uncle Bud. When they got off the phone, Mum told Father about her conversation with Jasmine and Wendy heard her mum telling her father. Today, Mum and Jasmine are good friends again. They even went to church together on this past Sunday.

Wendy includes in the conversation some final details to display the importance of her and Julie's friendship. Wendy supposes that Mum and Jasmine could have been better friends all along if Jasmine thought she could have trusted Mum to discuss her feelings about what happened to her. It was possible that Jasmine thought that Mum never said anything because at first Jasmine had a crush on Uncle Bud. But after that happened, Jasmine disliked Uncle Bud, Wendy said.

"Julie, if you have any secrets. Please, don't feel you have to hide anything from me. Julie, you can trust me! Tell me anything. I won't hold it against you or think anything strange. Okay?" Wendy asks.

"Yeah," Julie says quietly and turns her face away. I wonder if Wendy can handle a real secret. I understand how Jasmine must have felt. There are some things that are too hard to tell even your best friend. There is one thing I never told Wendy. It is a secret I'm not sure Wendy will understand because I don't understand it myself, Julie thinks.

"Now Julie, I really mean it! You can trust me with any secret and I won't tell anybody! Let's promise that we'll always be friends like they say at church: 'until Jesus comes back!' And that means forever! No matter where we live!" Wendy says, as she looks Julie directly in the eye.

"I promise we will be friends until Jesus comes back. Okay?" Julie repeats reluctantly and shifts her eyes away again. In the back of Julie's mind, she thinks about the one secret she is afraid to tell anybody.

Wendy looks at her watch. They have only seven minutes to get back home. Jumping up and walking fast, they quickly plan what to wear to school the next day, anything red: Julie's old favorite color. They finish their homework as Julie's mama, Pam, arrives to pick her up around 6:30 p.m. Riding home in the car while listening to a gospel tape, Julie is very quiet. She is glad that her mama is preoccupied with listening and singing along with the songs on the tape so she can think.

Julie considers what she and Wendy have discussed. She wants to keep her promise to Wendy but who can be trusted these days? Contemplating her decision, Julie ponders also what her mama always says about friendships. Mama says,

"You can't tell your friends everything 'cause some

friends aren't real friends. They can't be trusted. Whatever you tell them might end up on one of those television talk show programs. And then you'll be hurt because somebody, who you thought was a friend, broke a trust. There are so many people trying to make money off of other people's misery. Other friends, who are real friends, won't understand everything you go through. So, it's best to not tell people all your business."

Julie isn't sure she completely understands what her mama was talking about because her mama does not allow her to watch any talk shows where they tell people's personal business and secrets.

Julie decides. I can wait to tell Wendy my secret. I'm not sure Wendy can handle it. Although, I feel Wendy is a true friend and wants to remain friends with me, I'm afraid that Wendy may not really understand like Wendy says she will. Julie thinks.

Chapter 2
Julie's Secret

After they get home from Wendy's house, Mama puts her red car in the garage. Mama rushes in the house to finish dinner and listens to the voice mail. Daddy is not home yet. Mama slows down once she hears Daddy's message that he's gonna be coming home late and won't make it for dinner. Daddy had an unexpected business meeting again tonight. This is the third one in the same week. Looking worried at first, Mama changes her facial expression. She smiles. Mama tells Julie they will have pizza instead since Daddy is eating out.

After eating Julie and Mama settle down to watch television. Mama really likes to watch this particular program since it makes her laugh. Julie thinks it's funny too. Mama just came from the beauty shop the day before. The beautician placed Mama's reddish brown hair on rods so that the curls will stay in for a while. So every time Mama laughs, she throws her medium brown face backward, squints her eyes shut and her reddish brown curls bounce buoyantly. Julie is glad she has reddish brown hair like her mama's. Only Julie's hair is naturally curly.

When the program ends, it is 9 p.m. Mama tells Julie to prepare for bed. Daddy is still not home. Julie goes into her room and changes into her pajamas. Mama lets Julie read a chapter or two from the current book of the week she is reading and a little in Julie's own personal Bible every night. Mama always makes sure that Julie gets a new book from the library each week. Mama says that reading sharpens the mind.

Around 10 o'clock, Mama checks in on Julie. Mama

tells Julie to say her prayers and turn out her lights. Daddy is still not home yet. Julie thinks about her conversation earlier with Wendy. So, it takes a while even after the lights are out for Julie to go to sleep. After some time and as she feels her eyes getting heavy, Julie hears a car door slam. That must be Daddy she thinks. Oh, he finally came home. She hears Mama's footsteps coming from out of her parent's bedroom to meet him. I'll see Daddy in the morning, Julie thinks. Right now, I'm going to sleep.

Something shatters sounding like glass on the floor. The noise jolts Julie out of her twilight sleep.

"**SO, WHAT'S HIS NAME, PAM**?" shouts Julie's father, Julio.

"**I DON'T KNOW WHAT YOU'RE TALKING ABOUT!**" screams Pam.

Hearing the loud voices of her parents, the crash of something like a lamp breaking in the living room, and footsteps running in the hallway outside of her bedroom, Julie jumps up from her warm bed and runs to her bedroom door. Quickly, she locks the door. Grabbing her favorite red and black stuffed animal and her favorite signature blanket, Julie runs for her closet. Pulling that door closed also, she locks it. Shivering, Julie grasps the blanket and covers her head as tears stream down her face.

Julie's small body crunches in a corner of her closet on top of her old white designer sneakers, her red patent leather shoes and her black suede oxfords. Holding tightly to her favorite red and black stuffed animal, Julie shakes uncontrollably. Then Julie rocks herself. I want it to stop. I did what Mama says to do if I ever hear Daddy screaming at Mama. Why does he do this? It's happening again, Julie thinks.

"God please, don't let my daddy kill my mama. I promise you I'll be a good girl. God please let Daddy stop. Jesus, why is this happening again?" Julie whispers.

The walls of their house are so paper-thin. It seems as if you are right in the same room, even though both doors are shut.

"WHAT'S WRONG WITH YOU? WHY ARE YOU DOING THIS? JUST LEAVE ME ALONE! I DIDN'T DO ANYTHING!" Mama yells.

"LEAVE YOU ALONE! WHY? SO YOU CAN SLEEP WITH YOUR NEW MAN. WHO IS IT? THE NEW MAIL MAN? ¿CUÁL ES SU NOMBRE?" Daddy screams.

"JULIO! I'M NOT SLEEPIN' WITH ANYBODY! AND I DON'T CARE, WHO YOU'RE SLEEPIN' WITH. I'M NOT SLEEPIN' WITH ANYBODY! NOBODY BUT YOU, JULIO! HOW COME YOU CAN'T UNDERSTAND THAT?" Mama screams.

Whack! A loud thud vibrates the wall of Julie's bedroom. Sw-whack!

"I'LL MAKE SURE YOU WON'T SLEEP WITH HIM FOR A WEEK! WHEN I GET THROUGH WITH YOU, PAM, ¡ÉL NO TE QUERRÁ MÁS!" Daddy yells.

"OW! STOP HITTIN' ME, JULIO! I TOLD YOU, I'M NOT SLEEPIN' WITH NOBODY! WHY DON'T YOU BELIEVE ME! STOP IT! STOP IT! STOP IT!" Mama yells.

Julie sobs louder and pushes her fingers into the ears. She needs to drown out the noise she doesn't want to hear. She is so scared. At the top of her voice, Julie screams:

JESUS LOVES ME THIS I KNOW,
FOR THE BIBLE TELLS ME SO.
LITTLE ONES TO HIM BELONG,
THEY ARE WEAK BUT HE IS STRONG.

YES, JESUS LOVES ME.
YES, JESUS LOVES ME.
YES, JESUS LOVES ME
FOR THE BIBLE TELLS ME SO.

Jesus loves me this I know,
For the Bible tells me so.
Little ones to him belong,
They are weak but he is strong.

Yes, Jesus loves me.
Yes, Jesus loves me.
Yes, Jesus loves me
For the Bible tells me so.

Over and over, Julie shouts the song at first so she does not hear anything. After a while, she repeats the song softly. Julie feels better. Her tears began to dry and her body stops shaking. After a while, she calms down enough to fall asleep.

The next morning, Julie wakes up in the dark closet. Afraid at first, she starts to cry then she remembers why she's in the closet. Slowly, Julie stretches her arms and pulls her legs out from under her body. Her favorite red and black stuffed animal is lying on top of her brown cowgirl boots in the opposite corner. She threw him over there during the night. Cautiously, she opens the closet door.

The bright sunlight shines through her red and white striped signature curtains. Julie walks over to the window. Their gray luxury car is missing from the driveway, which means Daddy already went to work as a salesman for his company. Simultaneously, a knock comes at her bedroom door.

"Julie... Julie, honey, you can open the door now. Your

daddy's gone to work," Mama says.

"Okay, Mama," she says as she quickly unlocks her bedroom door.

Unlocking the door, Julie gasps. Her pretty mama's left eye is swollen and almost shut. Dried blood is on her plush pink robe, which is torn at the shoulder. A few buttons are missing. Mama's hair is sticking straight up on top of her head and matted on the sides. Tears fill Julie's eyes as she realizes that Mama is having a difficult time standing up.

"Oh, Mama! Why does he do this? Your pretty hair style is destroyed! I don't understand! I hate him! Mama, are you all right?" Julie asks as huge tears uncontrollably flow down her face. As she reaches out to touch her mama's side to support her, Mama gasps and pushes her away.

"Ow! No, baby. That hurts. Let me do it myself. I'm gonna be all right. I just need to sit down for a moment," Mama says softly as she holds her head with one hand. Walking slowly to Julie's bed and easing herself down, Mama focuses her right opened eye on Julie and says,

"Baby, don't cry. And, you can't hate your daddy, God don't like that. You'll have to forgive your daddy, you hear. Daddy needs Jesus in his life. So pray for him. We, you and I, need to talk. You can't stay home this time. I'm gonna let you go to school today."

"I did pray for him and you. Oh, Mama, I need to stay home and take care of you. Please, Mama. I wanna make sure you're all right," Julie pleads, blinking back the tears. Next Julie wipes her face to remove her tears.

"No, Julie, you're gonna go to school today. I've already called Mrs. King. She's coming over to help me. We'll pick you up from school today so don't get on the school bus after school, okay? Mrs. King is coming over here right after school starts. She'll help me clean up this house so you won't have to. Now, go get washed up for school. And don't forget to say your prayers, 'cause I'm still alive and Jesus didn't let me die. You keep praying for your daddy and me. I'll have Mrs. King here with me all day so you won't have to worry," Mama says to Julie as she reaches over and kisses her baby's soft brown face.

"Oh, Mama! You sure, Mama?" Julie asks.

"I'm sure, honey," says Pam.

Changing the subject to get her daughter's mind off of what happened, Pam asks Julie:

"What are you gonna wear to school today? And where is your favorite red and black stuffed animal?"

Wiping her face, Julie says:

"Oh, he's in the closet. He slept in the closet with me last night. I remembered to sing to myself just like you told me to. When I sang about Jesus, I felt better. Mama I think I'll wear my red designer sweater over my red jeans with my red designer socks and my red patent leather shoes under my red short winter jacket. Wendy and I decided our color today would be red. Mama, you don't need to fix my hair. I'll brush it myself. Okay?" Julie says. Kneeling beside her bed, Julie says her prayers. She remembers to thank God that her mama is still alive.

Getting up from the floor, she walks to the dresser to get her red and white designer underwear. She has to keep a good face in front of Mama so that Mama won't start crying like she did that one time. Julie remembers how her mama cried for three days. It was as if Mama was rehearsing in her mind that Daddy hit her in front of Julie. So every time Mama looked at Julie, she started crying all over again. Julie does not like it when her mama cries. So whenever Mama started crying, then Julie would cry. Next, they would be sitting in the front room holding each other and crying together. The second day after Daddy hit Mama; Mama's eyes were swollen so much from all that crying that she had to wear large dark sunglasses for a week whenever she left the house. Julie thinks.

Julie thinks of another time her daddy hit her mama. Then Mama only had her jaw swollen. Mama used to cuss at her daddy whenever he hit her. And Mama walked with no problem. Back then, Mama had not changed. Mama did not have Jesus living in her heart.

But this time: this time is terrible! This time Mama has Jesus living in her heart and Daddy really beat Mama bad! It is almost as if knowing Jesus does not make a difference. But that's not true because this time Julie did not find Mama crying on the couch unable to talk like she did one other time. Mama does have a problem walking but she is still alive! And Mama still has not used any cuss words, yet! Julie has to make sure she does not cry any more in front of Mama because she does not want to start Mama crying.

Opening her bedroom door, Julie hesitates for a moment before continuing down the hallway. There is a huge bloodstain on the wall outside of her bedroom and on the white carpet next to the wall. That must have been where Mama hit the wall last night, Julie thinks.

Glancing toward the living room, not only are the lamps shattered on the floor, but the blonde wood end-tables are upside down. Julie heads down the hall and goes into the common bathroom. Julie wonders: what does her parent's bathroom look like?

Closing the bathroom door, she runs warm shower water. Julie undresses. She puts on a shower cap. She grabs soap, her washcloth, steps into the shower, and washes her body. When she finishes, she dries off, quickly puts on clean underwear and brushes her teeth. Julie does not want to give her mama any problems today.

She goes back to her bedroom, hangs her pajamas up and puts her dirty underwear in the dirty clothes hamper outside her closet. She talks with Mama one more time. Mama is still sitting in the same spot Julie left her in before she washed up. Julie gets dressed for school and brushes her hair. Mama tells Julie to get some extra money out of Mama's purse for breakfast so that Julie may have the treat of eating breakfast in school. Julie tells Mama she loves her and will see her after school in the front of the building.

Leaving for school at 7 a.m. to catch her bus with Wendy at 7:08 a.m., Julie thinks again about Wendy and her conversation from the day before. Should I tell Wendy my secret? As my friend, can I count on Wendy to help me hate my daddy? Or would Wendy pray for me because my family is in trouble?

I cannot tell Wendy. Wendy will tell her mum. Then maybe Wendy's mum will tell the people at the church. Then *everybody* will know our business! Somebody might even call one of those talk shows; get on the show and tell the whole world. NO! This is one secret I will not tell Wendy. We'll stay friends without this secret being shared. I'll have to be somewhat like Jasmine and keep this secret to myself. There will be other secrets Wendy and I can share and still be friends. Julie thinks.

Chapter 3
The Plan

Sometime after Julie leaves for school, Pam struggles to her feet. She realizes she is having difficulty standing. Steadying herself, she keeps from falling by leaning on the walls. Pam slowly makes her way to the living room. She carefully steps around the huge chunks of furniture strewn all over the floor. Inching her body slowly down onto the plush couch, Pam sits on the softest place available, where her wounds do not hurt as much.

Pam places a hand to her throbbing head. Her mind wanders. "If I think too hard about why this happened, I'll start crying again. I don't have time for that now. No, I must stay focused," Pam thinks. "I already have one eye I can barely see out of. I don't need both of them swollen from crying too hard. Then I won't be able to see at all. I'm sleepy and I've got to stay awake to let Sister King in."

Pam looks at the time. It is 8:10 a.m. She realizes that Sister King might need some help because this time she is not able to do any work. Her back is hurting. Her lip is split. Her body aches all over. Pam remembers how hard she hit the wall the night before.

Glancing around the room, Pam locates the blue telephone, which is off the hook. Holding her head with one hand and struggling to pull her weight forward, Pam balances herself first on the edge on the deep cushion of the couch then gradually stands up. Leaning on the arm of the couch, the only thing that Julio did not turn upside down in the living room, she steadies herself in place. Keeping her back straight, Pam bends her knees and eases her way down into a squatting position. She knows from previous situations like this that it is best not to bend forward because her head will hurt worse. Pulling the base of the telephone toward her, Pam slowly retrieves the handset. Once she places the handset on the base of the telephone; Pam can make her telephone call.

As she listens for a dial tone, a double tone beeps indicating that Pam has a message. Maybe Sister King tried to call her back. Pam pretended to be asleep since she was afraid to move until she heard the screech of Julio's tires when he left for work earlier this morning. Once Julio was gone, Pam called Sister King with her cell phone from her purse near the bed. Her cell phone could easily be slipped back into her purse, just in case she heard Julio doubling back. Occasionally, he did and she didn't want him to find her on the regular telephone talking with anyone. That only leads to more confrontation. Dialing their voice mail, she listens to the messages before she calls Sister King.

The first message:

"Hey, Sister Pam, this is Sister Toni King. I was prayin' and feel we'll really need more than one person to help us clean your house. I just wanna let you know we do have at International Church, some women, whom are experienced in workin' with your type of situation. They've handled cases like these many times before. They're part of our Victorious Living Ministry Team. You don't hear a lot about them because only the pastor and those in real need, find out, who they are.

"So I wanna let you know that I'm bringin' Sister Desireé, Sister Irene and Sister Sheri with me. This type of thing happens. Our team is diverse 'cause it don't matter what walk of life the woman comes from or what nationality a woman is, she's able to identify and talk with at least one member of our team in comfort. We'll arrive somewhere close to 8:30 a.m. Now, don't you worry about nothin' and don't try to do nothin' until we get there. We'll take care of everythin'. And Sister Pam, these women know how to keep a secret. Your business is safe with them. I know mine has been. Love, ya!"

Pressing the number five key, the voice mail reveals the call was received at 7:02 a.m. and it is a minute and 30 seconds long. Smiling for a moment, Pam thinks. "Those women from the church: they really work fast! So this is the church ministry Sister Toni's involved in. And these other women must be Sister Toni's prayer partners."

She presses the number seven key to delete the message. Pam does not want Julio to pick up the message and find out she is getting help to clean the house. Pam knows the house must be cleaned before Julio comes home or he might go into a rage again.

Feeling a throbbing pain from her bent legs, Pam cautiously eases onto the couch and avoids splattered broken glass on the floor. She listens to message number two.

The second message:

"Pam honey, it's me. You must not be answerin' 'cause the phone is off the hook. I must've done that last night. I wanna apologize. I don't know what got into me. I'm really sorry! Really, I am! It won't happen again. Are you okay? I didn't mean to hurt you. Baby, you know I really love you! How's Julie this morning? You know I didn't see her last night. Did she get off to school okay?

"Listen honey: Sweetie-cakes, I've got to go out of town on business. I'll be leavin' today at 11:06 a.m. with the airlines we normally use here on the job on flight 144 to San Francisco, CA. I have to negotiate a contract with one our oldest clients. You know, Sweetie-cakes, I'm really sorry. Baby, this job is so stressful! But it brings in the big bucks! Maybe I was stressed out about makin' this trip. It's a really big one and they just told me last night. You know how I hate short notices and changes. And you know how I like to take you and Julie with me everywhere I go. Well, this time I couldn't.

"I sent you some yellow flowers to show how sorry I am. They should cheer you up and keep you company. I'll call you once my flight gets in this afternoon. Julie should be home by then. Let's see, today's Tuesday. I won't be back in town until next Monday. There're some other people I'm supposed to meet and network with until Sunday evening. Mr. Johnson wants me to keep the clients happy. I'll see you and Julie early Monday afternoon. Then I'll take you guys, my women, out on the town. We'll go shopping. I'll buy you anything you want and really make up for what happened last night.

"Hon, I've got some reports to work on before I go. The company's limousine is picking me up at 9:00 a.m., so don't call the office because I won't be available. I love you, Pam. You're the only one for me."

Pam frowns as she presses the number five key. The voice mail reveals the call was received at 7:04 a.m. Julio called right after Sister Toni did, so he didn't have time to check the messages because he was so busy leaving his message. Pam is glad she deleted that message from Sister Toni before Julio decided to check all the messages as he had in times past.

Tears form in her eyes as Pam realizes she got beat

up because of an unscheduled business trip! Julio hates surprises. He probably had some plans in our city that had to be changed because of this short notice business trip. Once Julio establishes his plans, he does not like rearranging anything. Pam remembers the day they were to go to a baseball game in the middle of July before Julie was born.

****

Julio walked up the driveway to their apartment building. Turning the key in the door, he sauntered through the doorway with a spring in his step.

"Pam, you ready for our big date to the baseball game. I haven't been to a baseball game in over five years. This is really gonna be great! I've got some big pillows and a soft cushion for you to sit on. I even remembered to pick up a few oversized umbrellas so that you won't get sunburned, just in case your skin is sensitive to sittin' in the sun," Julio called out as he walked from the living room into their bedroom.

"Julio, I don't think I can make it to the baseball game today. I can barely walk and my back is hurting something terrible," Pam said as she bent forward in the chair. Clutching her back with one hand, she blew air through her oval shaped lips. Simultaneously, she mentally counted how long that pain lasted.

"What do you mean, you can't make the game? You know how long I've been plannin' this outing for us? I got off work special so that we could spend this afternoon together and now you're havin' pains?" he shouted. He plopped down on their bed next to his starched faded blue jeans and his ironed favorite signature baseball tee shirt she laid out for him.

Breathing deeply as the pain subsided, Pam looked

at her watch. She realized it was exactly 15 minutes since the last pain. The doctor warned Pam that if the pains are any closer than 20 minutes apart to come in right away. Since she was a high-risk patient, he had been watching her all along. Pam lost their first baby through a miscarriage and the doctor didn't want to take any chances with her life nor this baby's life.

"Well, honey, I called the doctor's office and he wants me to meet him at the hospital. You can go to the game without me. I'll just call Big Dee and see if he can take me to the hospital," she replied.

"You ain't gonna be callin' nobody. Why did you have to get a man doctor in the first place? The baby ain't due until next month. So, he wants you to meet him at the hospital, uh. Not without me bein' there! I'll call your brother myself to see if he can use these tickets. It's a shame, prime seats." Julio mumbled. Next, he said something Pam figured out some time later. He said it so sharply under his breath. "And I hate changin' my plans! I made those plans! They were my plans!"

He was so upset that his plans had been messed up. As they drove to the hospital, he accused her of wishing the baby was born on that day just to mess his plans up and inconvenience him on purpose. She was glad the hospital admitted her for the next 10 days. It was too early for Julie to come and her doctor wanted her off her feet in the bed. The time she spent in the hospital helped Julio calm down. He realized some things are unavoidable, especially when a baby is involved.

He visited her every day to make sure nobody else was looking at his wife. At first, she thought this jealousy thing was cute until Julio was ridiculously nasty to the male nurse, who relieved her regular female nurse. Julio was so rude to the male nurse that the man refused to relieve her regular female nurse again the entire time she was there.

Julio's attitude with that old jealousy streak softened and disappeared for a while once Julie was born. It was like he was his old self. The man she fell in love with, who was tenderhearted and thoughtful. Not abusive. During that time, he never hit her. He became that joyful man, who courted her, wooed her and won her love again and again.

****

Him having to go out of town unexpectedly, and being very suspicious probably activated his old ugly jealousy streak and distorted his judgment. Well, Pam thinks. I can take my time cleaning the house. As streams of salty tears run down her face, they sting the split skin of her lip. Pam breaks into sobs thinking about the whole situation. She says out loud.

"Flowers to keep me company? Sorry? He's not sorry! He beat me the last time he went out of town! And at that point he promised he wouldn't do it again. He said then it was because I asked too many questions. I was pressurin' him. I was stressin' him out. But I know he hit me because he doesn't want me out of the house while he's gone. He doesn't want anybody lookin' at me. That's why he is always accusin' me of being with somebody else. Why does he do this? He knows I'm faithful to him. I don't love nobody else." Pam sits still for a while thinking of what to do next to end this situation.

Focusing on God, Pam prays out loud.

"God, I don't believe he loves me. He can't love me. Father God, you said real love doesn't hurt people like this. He said he was sorry the last time! He always says: 'He's sorry' and does it again. God, I don't wanna go through this again. Please, God show me what to do! I need your help. I'm tired of this. I can't take it no more. I don't wanna be hit again. I need to know: what do I do? I really..."

Just then the doorbell rings. The sound hurts Pam's head.

"Who is it?" Pam calls out.

"Sister Pam. It's us. We made it," Sister Toni replies.

"Just a minute… I'm a little slow… I'm coming… I'll be there in a moment," Pam says. She methodically gathers enough strength to get up off the couch. Pam stands straight up being careful not to bend forward. Feeling lightheaded, she cautiously moves toward the door leaning on the couch to keep her balance and making sure not to step on glass so that it will not go through her soft house slippers.

After Pam turns the lock, she steps back behind the wooden door out of the bright sunlight and lets in the four women from her church. Sister Toni, a 4'10" Hispanic, takes over the responsibility of closing and locking the door. The other three women sigh in shock over the condition of the house. Sister Toni's shoulder length hair swishes as she rapidly turns her head to focus on why the other women react the way they do. Sister Sheri reaches out to steady Pam but Pam pulls away from her.

"I can do it, Sister Sheri. If you help me, it'll hurt. I'm glad you brought the other sisters with you. I'm in so much pain I can't do anything," she says.

"Well, Sister Pam, you needs to sit down and rest. I wanna talk to you, anyway," Sister Sheri says. Sister Sheri is a medium brown skinned African American woman with long silver hair. She is dressed in a maxi blue jean skirt with a blue tee shirt. Pam has never seen Sister Sheri wear pants. She and Pam are about the same height.

As Pam makes her way back to the couch; Sister Toni collects all their jackets and hangs them up in the closet. Sisters Irene and Desireé turn over the lounge chair, the loveseat, and the ottoman into their upright positions. Sister Irene is a Caucasian blonde, about 5'10" with a short bob haircut. She is wearing black slacks and an oversized black tee shirt. Sister Desireé, who is a little shorter than Sister Irene, has her coal black hair pinned in a bun on top of her head. She always wears her traditional Indian Shalwar kameez. Today hers has a purple background with large flowers over purple pants.

Sister Toni goes into the kitchen to get a paper bag, broom and dust pan so she can sweep up the glass from the broken lamps. Part of their ministry training is to allow one person to speak with the victim. The other sisters of the team clean the home and softly pray for God to give wisdom to the person speaking.

These women decided before they arrived to leave all the talking this time to Sister Sheri since she was in this situation herself years ago. Quickly, they move around the house straightening and arranging things into their proper places. These women had been to this home before for a few social events when things were not as tense and know how immaculate Sister Pam keeps her home.

As Pam settles in on the couch, Sister Sheri sits down next to her gently so that she does not jar the couch.

"Sister Pam, first of all, I know us knowin' about this here situation ain't easy for you. And I thinks you needs to go to the hospital. You could have a concussion," Sister

Sheri says. She sweeps her silvery hair back from her medium brown face and waits for Sister Pam to respond. Sister Sheri thinks: "Sister Pam looks terrible. She's barely able to keep her head up and one eye looks like it's almost completely shut. Sister Pam may have some nerve damage to her eye."

Pam sits still on the couch for a moment. It hurts to shake or move her head in any direction. Her back hurts. Her balance is off. And Pam just wants this whole thing to be over.

"Well, Sister Sheri, I'm glad y'all came. I may need some help getting dressed. I really appreciate what you ladies are doing. I don't think I could make it through today or these next few days without your help.

"In terms of my situation, I know I need to do something. And I know I need to go to the hospital. But I don't want them to keep me, especially since I've decided I can't take this anymore! I wanna do something but I really don't know what to do!" Pam responds. Her voice rises a little at the end as if she is trying to convince herself.

"Sister Pam, I don't like to do this but I feel this is the reason why I'm here today. I is gonna share my story. I was prayin' and readin' my Bible. God reminded me how He used someone to talk to me 19 years ago when I was goin' through problems with my first husband." Sister Sheri says.

"A church mother in my old church talked to me a week before my first husband beat me that one last time. She'd been in the same situation. She used to be beaten by her husband and she gave me the same scripture verse I was readin' this mornin'. I know you reads the New International Bible (NIV). I memorized it from the King James

Bible (KJV). The scriptures are 2 Corinthians 1:3 and 4, which say:

> *"Blessed be God, even the Father of our Lord Jesus Christ, the Father of mercies, and the God of all comfort; Who comforteth us in all our tribulation, that we may be able to comfort them which are in any trouble, by the comfort wherewith we ourselves are comforted of God" (2 Corinthians 1:3-4 KJV).*

"When I got the telephone call from Sister Toni that you is in trouble, I felt God tellin' me to come talk with you. I had somethin' else to do. But God had me to come here with you today because you needs my help, Sister Pam. It's my turn to comfort somebody else," Sister Sheri says.

"You knows how God is. He uses some peoples to give us advance warnin's of danger. My first husband used to beat me so regularly that all five of our children hid ever' time Daddy came home. The week before the church mother gave me this verse my first husband had given me a black eye. She told me then it was time for me to leave. She was my warnin' and I didn't listen. I was so scared. I'd been a housewife for 14 years and didn't know how to work a job outside the home.

"The last time he beat me was 19 years ago a week after that church mother gave me that warnin'. He hit me so many times that I was curled up on the floor in a fetal position. I was screamin'. My children were cryin'. I was prayin' he'd stop. When he heard me pray, he began kickin' me. That's when I blacked out. I woke up as the paramedics were takin' me by ambulance to the hospital. I stayed in the hospital three whole weeks. My left eye was closed shut. I had two stitches in the corner of it. I had internal bleeding, a punctured lung and a swollen spleen," Sister Sheri says.

Sister Pam interrupts, "No, not a swollen spleen."

"Yes, a swollen spleen, he probably did it when he was kickin' me. But three weeks is a long time. It gave me time to think. Think about how I didn't have to wake up," Sister Sheri says.

Sister Pam interrupts again, "Did he ever apologize? Say, he was sorry?"

"Oh, ever' time he'd apologize. Say he was sorry. He even brought yellow roses to the hospital to apologize. Then he promise it wouldn't happen again. But I realized they was only words he gotten used to sayin'," Sister Sheri says.

"I know what you mean," Pam interjects meekly.

"He'd buy me new clothes 'cause he ripped up my old clothes while they were on my body in his anger, rage and jealousy. He'd take me on shoppin' sprees. After a while, his money and gifts couldn't compensate for my internal pain and wounds. Those things didn't measure up.

"We'd been married for 14 years. I'd stayed in the marriage for the sake of the children. At least, that's what I told myself. Sittin' in the hospital, I realized how violent our children had gotten lately. The worse was our oldest son: Jacob. He tormented his sisters and brothers. He picked up those same vicious spirits of jealousy, anger and rage his daddy had. Jacob even lost a girlfriend because of his intense jealousy. Jacob began disrespecting me. I didn't want Jacob actin' like his daddy," Sister Sheri says.

"Lyin' in the hospital bed, I remembered my lifelong friend, Winnie. Winnie and I were best friends from 5th grade. We stayed friends as adults. Winnie's husband abused her too. She didn't live after her husband beat her up the last time. Winnie died on the operatin' table. Winnie's husband went to jail for involuntary manslaughter while her relatives raised Winnie's only son," Sister Sheri says.

"She died?" Pam asks in disbelief.

"Yeah, Winnie died. We'd been through everythin' together: prom, datin', and graduatin' from high school. We'd even worked at the same job until she went off to college and I got married. The memory of Winnie and the realization of where I was at at that moment kinda brought me around. I had time to realize, although this was the worst time, I might not live the next time. I had five children and I couldn't take that chance. I mean it finally struck me and stuck out in my mind: *What if I didn't wake up?* **He almost killed me!** What would happen to my children? I decided right then, it was time for me to leave and take the children with me!" Sister Sheri says.

Sister Sheri suggests to Sister Pam that perhaps she can look into a shelter for battered women and children. If Sister Pam calls the crisis hot line, they can arrange a secluded place out of the county that is safe away from her husband.

"But if we're out of the county, Julie would have to be taken out of the school in this area and that would break her heart. She's so close with Wendy. They've been friends for years. What would I tell Wendy's mother, Cindy? She and I have been friends since Wendy and Julie were 3 years old. She doesn't know about my problems with Julio. I'm not sure I can take Julie away from her friends and school. Besides, Julio wouldn't be foolish enough to follow me anywhere," Pam says confidently.

"That's the way I thought at first. I moved into the shelter closest to my children's schools to keep them with their friends. I made arrangements with another person at the shelter to pick up my children from their schools and take different routes to deliver them to the shelter. I listened to the warnin' I got from the counselor at the shelter. I got a court order, which stated: only I had temporary legal custody of our children. A copy of it was on file at my children's schools. The people at the shelter tried to move me to a shelter located out of the area... out of the county. That warnin' I didn't listen to. I thought I knew best! I figured with the changes the children were goin' through at least their schools would be stable for them," Sister Sheri says.

"My first husband discovered they were still goin' to the same schools. He showed up randomly at the children's schools harassin' them trying to get our children to tell him where the shelter was. We had to get the police involved. Then he tried to follow the children to the shelter. Next, my first husband tried to transfer them out of their schools and move them out of state. He couldn't do anythin' 'cause I had that court order on file with the schools," Sister Sheri says.

"After that, my first husband told Jacob that he'd kill me before he would let anyone else be with me. Jacob tried to tackle his father. Fortunately, the security guard at Jacob's school remembered my first husband from one of the earlier incidents and had called the city police when my ex-husband entered the building. They arrived before Jacob's daddy did too much damage to him," Sister Sheri says.

"It was then I realized that not only was I in danger but my children too! I agreed to move to a shelter out of the county. It was the best thin' I could have done! All my children received counselin'. And right now today, they love their daddy, do not hate him and pray for him. Jacob's married to a sweet woman. And my first grandbaby is on the way," Sister Sheri replies softly.

"You don't think Julio would hurt Julie?" Pam asks with a frown on her face.

"You only have one daughter. Do you want to take that chance? Besides, you ain't said you even decided to leave Julio? This here is a moot point if you ain't decided to leave. Right now, I thought we is only talkin' about takin' you to the hospital. I told you about my situation. The decision must be yours. I don't wanna push you into anythin'. I wanna make sure you understand all the options and the process because it's not an easy road to travel. There're risks involved," Sister Sheri says.

Sister Sheri talks about how difficult it was to go from a hefty income to no income. She struggled so long with little or no money. At first, she received food stamps. She did not like it but it was worth it for the mental health of her children and herself. Eventually, in the process of the divorce proceedings, Sister Sheri found a job.

Sister Irene removes a small disposable camera from her pocket and takes pictures. She does this before she washes Pam's blood off the wall and off the white carpet next to that wall. Until this point, Pam had not noticed the camera since she was so engrossed in conversation with Sister Sheri. Sister Irene asks Sister Pam if she may take pictures of her just in case, she decides to press charges at a later time. Pam agrees. When Sister Irene snaps the camera for the pictures, the flash from the camera hurts her almost closed left eye. "Me! Press charges against Julio?" I wonder if I could even do that. I'm so scared of him. Pam thinks.

Julio was not always violent like this. Pam's mind races to remember when it all started. Oh, yeah, something snapped in Julio's head around the time Julie turned three. I used to take Julie shopping by train to downtown Chicago and to the museums. Julie was potty-trained and traveled real easy. It was during that time Julio's old jealousy streak returned. Only it didn't return like it had been in times past, his jealously thing returned with a vengeance, Pam thinks.

It started with a simple slap because he thought I looked at some man or because I returned a smile to some man. From that point on, I do not look directly in any man's face. That strategy has worked for a while, Pam thinks.

"Sister Pam... Sister Pam..." Sister Sheri interrupts Pam's thoughts.

"Yes?" Pam responds.

"Sister Pam, I wonders if you decided? If you did then maybe I can helps you get dressed and into some street clothes instead of that nightgown before we go to the hospital. And I think we needs to get some fresh pictures of your body," Sister Sheri says.

"Oh, yes... I'm not sure about pressing charges... (pausing for a long time)... But I do wanna go to the hospital. And... (she pauses again) I wanna shower before I go," Pam replies.

"You do realize not everyone showers in a situation like this before they go to the Emergency Room at the hospital," Sister Sheri says.

"I know but I wanna put on fresh underwear in case they keep me," Sister Pam says.

"Okay, it's your choice," Sister Sheri says.

Pam struggles to get off the couch. Sister Sheri remembers not to help her. Sister Sheri stands behind Sister Pam just in case she loses her balance. Sister Irene gives Sister Sheri the camera.

Slowly, Sister Sheri follows Pam into her bedroom. Sister Toni has changed the sheets and is in the process of finishing making up the bed when they walk in. Pam trudges toward the master bathroom, which is larger than the common bathroom. Sister Sheri follows her with the camera. Once Pam disrobes, Sister Sheri takes pictures.

Sister Sheri does not like this part of the work, looking at how badly these women have been beaten. Purple bruises are forming around Sister Pam's stomach area. Her arms and legs are bluish-black. A large black ring forms around her left eye. If Sister Pam didn't make up her mind to leave now, she might not live the next time. Sister Pam is a brown skinned woman. Julio must have hit her pretty hard several times in the same place for her brown skin to turn bluish-black this fast.

Black people's bruises with her skin shade of brown don't show easily or quickly. It is usually through x-rays, ultra sounds and medical examinations that it is discovered how badly they are injured. Sister Pam is putting on a brave front because Sister Sheri knows Sister Pam is in some serious pain.

Sister Sheri soaps up the wash cloth for Pam as she stands in the shower. Sister Sheri stands outside the shower stall with a big towel, just in case, Pam needs her help. Pam is glad Sister Sheri is there. Pam takes things slowly from there and continues her thoughts. "When is the first time this happened?"

****

The first real time Julio beat her was after a company Christmas party. She wore a tight-fitting, low-cut black dress. She had been exercising and finally gotten all that baby fat off from carrying Julie. All the men from his job tried to dance with her the entire time she and Julio were there. Julio had been able to shoo them away, but not his boss.

Julio's boss danced at least five times with her. Each time Julio's boss asked him for a dance with his wife, Julio drank a little more. Julio was afraid to say no to his boss like he did his co-workers. It did not help that each time the boss danced with her, Julio listened to his co-workers teasing him about how the boss may want to get Julio's fine wife in his bed. They were only playing with him but they did not know the dark side of Julio. He could not take joking about anything especially his wife. Pam thinks.

Julie was at a friend's house that entire weekend, which was good. Because when they got home, Pam and Julio got into an argument. Julio accused her of purposely ruining his night and flirting with his boss. He hit her repeatedly in her face with his open palm to make sure it was bruised but not damaged. It took almost two weeks for her face to go back to normal. That was the last company party she agreed to go. She always stayed at home after that. And to make sure she was at home, Julio would call her every half an hour on the house phone. Pam thinks.

Pam was glad it happened that time early enough in December so by the time the holidays came, the makeup she wore covered the last few bruises that were still visible. She was also glad Julie was away the weekend it happened because Pam did not want Julie to see how bad she looked. Pam thinks.

Julio knew his boss was a womanizer and had slept

with a few of the other men's wives, which is how they got their promotions. Only these men did not know their boss was sleeping with their wives. Now, Julio had this jealousy thing combined with control because somehow he found out about his boss' infidelities.

****

Julio has to know every move I make. And the beatings have gotten progressively worse from that point on. I realize that I cannot continue to live like this. I may end up dead like Sister Sheri's friend, Winnie. Pam thinks.

Pam makes it safely out of the shower and sits on her bed. She feels a little lightheaded and is still in a lot of pain. Sister Desireé brings Pam some milk to drink to coat her stomach while she takes some pain medicine. She is unable to eat because she has no appetite. Struggling to keep the pain from getting worse, Sister Sheri helps Pam step into and pull up her clothes. In that moment, Pam decides to leave Julio. I need a plan. Pam fears for her life. **I have only one life and as damaged as it is, it is still precious to me**. Pam thinks. (Her thoughts race as Pam tries to figure everything out.)

But how could I leave the only man I really love? When Julio is kind, he is easy to talk to. He is sweet. It is only when he gets that alcohol in his system that he's mean. Maybe I just need a break from him. Things aren't too bad. What about all our property together? Can I leave everything? Pam thinks.

He still gives me complete access to all our accounts. He has not hit me in the last six months. And I love his smile. Pam softly prays so only God can hear her,

"Oh, God. What should I do?"

While Sister Pam seems lost in thought, Sister Sheri

prays to God softly under her breath.

"Father God, I know you can help Sister Pam. Please, don't let her be deceived into thinkin' that Julio won't do this again. I know he will and you know he will. Father, help Sister Pam to make the right decision. And God, could you work with Julie's mind, just in case, Sister Pam decides to leave her husband. You know how hard it was for my children. I wished I had someone prayin' for them. Please, Father God, get Julie ready for this possible change in her life in Jesus' name, Amen."

Immediately, Pam's thoughts change. Flashing back in time, Pam remembers the times Julio hit her and he had not been drinking. No alcohol at all: just rage, control and jealousy! I have access to all the accounts because he does not like to do the accounting and I'm better at it. Julio checks to make sure I pay everything on time, so he still keeps the ultimate control. And when was the last time I have really been able to talk about anything with Julio without the fear of him retaliating? I have to admit, I cautiously choose my words these days. I even must make sure Julie does not say the wrong thing to her daddy. Or I am blamed for it. Pam thinks.

What kind of love is that? I realize this is not my warm comfortable home any more. It is Julio's prison where I am the controlled inmate. And his smile looks devilish lately whenever he hits me. Sometimes Julio seems to enjoy inflicting pain on me. I recall seeing a twisted smile as he hit me last night. Does he really love me or love hurting me? Pam thinks.

No, I need to leave while he is out of town and unable to trace my steps so easily. But I need these women's help.

I can't leave without all of Julie's things, especially her favorite red and black stuffed animal and her favorite signature blanket. Pam thinks.

Pam decides to go to the hospital only after she is safely far enough away. Although her husband isn't returning for a week, Pam doesn't want to be stuck in a hospital close by just in case she's admitted. She talks it over with Sister Sheri as she continues dressing. Sister Sheri assures her that they will help her get medical attention.

Sister Sheri tells the members of the Victorious Living Ministry Team Sister Pam's decision to leave. The church women operate quickly cleaning the house and packing up Julie and Sister Pam's clothes. They're careful to get Julie's favorite red and black stuffed animal; her favorite signature blanket and Julie's favorite pillow. They know they have to finish everything quickly and get Sister Pam out of the house before Julio calls.

Sister Irene reminisces about another woman, who had decided to leave her abusive situation. Right at the moment of leaving that woman's house, her husband called. In fear and against their protests, the woman answered the telephone and listened to her husband say, "Baby, I'm sorry." The phone call changed that other woman's mind. Four years later, she is still being beaten up. She even came to church a few times with her arm in a sling or a cast. That woman does not have any front teeth, only dentures at 34 years old. All of Sister Pam's teeth are intact. Sister Toni took the telephone off the hook while Pam was in the bathroom washing her body to ensure no calls got through.

By the time the women finish packing as much as possible in Pam's matching purple suitcases, Julie's signature suitcases and some boxes; Pam manages to be completely dressed. She covers her head with a large scarf. She had assistance from Sister Sheri since Pam cannot easily slip her arms into her clothing. The boxes and suitcases are packaged in the trunk of the car and on the back seat. On top of one box on the backseat, so that Julie will be comfortable, are her favorite red and black stuffed animal, her favorite signature blanket and Julie's favorite pillow.

Pam picks up their checkbook, her oversized dark shades, a few of their major credit cards and keys to the safety deposit box. Pam incorporates this into the plan. She leaves her cell phone on the kitchen table after erasing all her contacts so that Julio cannot track her through her cell phone. I'll get another cell phone later, Pam thinks.

I am not leaving anything. I'm not going to be broke like Sister Sheri was. Listening to Sister Sheri taught me something. Pam thinks.

Sister Sheri retrieves everyone's jacket from the closet. Sister Irene helps Pam into her jacket and to her car. Finally, it doesn't hurt to lean on anyone. Sister Toni places the telephone on the hook. Closing the front door, Sister Desireé locks it. She hears the telephone ringing. The ministry team got Pam out just in time.

As Pam sits in the front seat of her car on the passenger side, Sister Toni drives Pam's car to the bank. At the bank, Pam removes 3/4ths of the available cash from Julio and hers' joint bank account. She decides to take it to a totally different bank and place it in an account with only her name on it. There is a bank across the street that has locations throughout the United States. She is sure wherever Julie and she end up; Pam will have access to this account. Pam decides to ask Sister Toni to drive her over there after she finishes everything here at this bank.

Next, she removes everything from the safety deposit box, places it in a large manila envelope, seals the envelope and puts it into her oversize purse. Pam decides to move this into a bank with a safety deposit box near the shelter. Sister Toni agrees to take her across the street. There Pam opens up a new account with only her name on it. Since the new bank is in competition with her old bank, Pam also receives a cash bonus for opening the new account. She assigns that all mail be sent to their church address. This way there will be no paper trail for Julio to discover.

Last but not least, it is getting close to the time to pick Julie up from school. They stop at Sister Sheri's house to call the Domestic Violence Crisis Hot Line. Pam gives Sister Toni the phone after she talks with them to write down the directions for getting to the women's shelter in another county. She cannot drive and needs Sister Toni to be able to locate her if necessary. Pam sits in the back seat for the rest of the trip. Laying her head on Julie's things, Pam relaxes. They stop to pick up some food. Pam wants to make sure Julie eats as they travel. Sister Irene, Sister Desiree and Sister Sheri follow them in Sister Sheri's red car. The last stop is Julie's school.

Sitting in the car in front of Julie's school with Sister Toni, Pam realizes all that has transpired in the last 16-17 hours. She is grateful these women can be trusted with her secret and her personal business.

"But, why did it have to come to this?" Pam thinks. She hears the answer clearly from God: something had to change. You can't live your life as you have in the past. You need to live and not die. At the rate things are going, you can't trust Julio with your life.

Trust... hummm. We, Julio and I, started out as friends. We trusted each other. Our friendship turned to love. What kind of love do we have now? And what kind of friendship do we have now? Julio proves to be a friend I can't trust. It is time to change friends or at least lose this friend. Pam thinks.

Change--something I did not think I would ever do-- has to happen. "Julio and I were supposed to be together forever. That's why we got married." Will I be brave enough to make these changes? I must do it for Julie and myself. These are necessary steps to take for our lives: for my life. Pam thinks.

Praying quietly so only God can hear her, Pam says, "Father God, I thank you for my life and for these women. Thank you for my church and their help. Please help Julie forgive me and understand, in Jesus' name amen."

Chapter 4
A Day of Surprises

While Julie stands at the bus stop waiting for the bus to come with the same two goofy boys: Jerry and Peter, who are always there, Wendy arrives. Peter pushes Jerry over into the bushes just as the bus pulls up. Jerry's red book bag flies into the dirt and he drops his paper lunch bag trying to keep his balance. Brushing the dirt from his book bag and his designer blue jeans, Jerry picks up his book bag with one hand and scoops up his lunch with his other hand.

Then Jerry shouts,

"Peter, man, I'm gonna get you for this! Look at what you did to my book bag!"

Laughing, Peter jumps on the bus and runs to the rear of it.

"'Cuse me," Jerry says as he pushes pass Wendy and Julie to run after Peter.

"Simmer down. And stop that running, you guys know the rules on this bus. There had better not be any fighting or both of you fellows will be written up," the driver says.

"You girls come along. We've got a schedule to keep," he tells Wendy and Julie.

Greeting other students on the bus, the two girls find seats together in the middle of the bus. Wendy's eyes glisten.

"I'm so glad I remembered to wear red like we planned yesterday," Wendy says. She is dressed in red overalls with a white short sleeved blouse trimmed in red under her white winter jacket. Wendy also has on a new pair of red gym shoes. Her hair is pulled up in a tight ponytail with a red ponytail holder.

"Wen, girl I'm glad you remembered too. Did you start your report due next Thursday?" Julie asks.

"No! But guess what!!! When Father came home last night, he had great news! Father's job is sending him to Florida on business almost a month from now. He's going to take us with him: Mum and me! I'm so excited! We'll be there a week and a half counting two Saturdays and two Sundays. We plan to go to that famous amusement park in Orlando, Florida three of those days!" Wendy exclaims as her freckled cheeks turned bright red.

"Girl, Wen! I'm not jealous. I'm not jealous. I wanna go too! But, I know I can't go! I'm so excited for you! Your dad's okay!" Julie says.

"Yeah, I know. Just think a vacation in the sun, by the pool, on the beach, near..."

Both Wendy and Julie high-five each other and say it at the same time,

"New guys!"

"New guys with tanned bodies," Julie says dreamingly.

"Yeah," Wendy sighs.

"Wen, girl when you get to the beach, make sure you take pictures, especially if you meet a fine one," Julie giggles.

"I will," Wendy giggles.

"But seriously, you know your mum is not gonna let any guy get within 15' of you. And you know what they always say..." Julie says as she looks directly in Wendy's eyes. In unison, they both say,

"You girls are only 12 so quit drooling! You have your entire life ahead of you. School's first! Boys come later!"

Laughing for a few minutes, Julie realizes laughing makes her feel better. As the laughing subsides, Julie changes the subject. She makes Wendy promise to bring back a souvenir from whichever amusement park they visit. The rest of the way to school, they talk about how great Wendy's father is for taking the whole family with him on this business trip.

Julie finds out that Wendy's father's job is going to pay for their hotel room in Orlando, FL, which includes breakfast. He only has to pay airfare for Wen's mum and Wendy to get there. Since it is a month away, Wendy's father called last night. He got their airplane tickets reserved. Wendy's mum is picking them up today. Wendy will miss school for only one week. It's okay since she is going to get homework from all her classes to take with her.

Julie bubbles with excitement because she is going to help Wendy plan her wardrobe. Maybe Julie will even loan Wendy a few of her skirts that look great on Wendy's long thin legs. Absorbed in Wendy's great news, Julie forgets completely about what happened at home last night.

When the girls get off the school bus, Wendy looks around her to see who is close by. Then she turns to Julie and says,

"Remind me at lunch today that I've got something to tell you. It's a secret. I almost forgot with all the excitement. If I don't tell you at lunch then maybe I can tell you at my house after school today. You can call your mama and ask her if you can come over again today."

"Oh, Wen, girl I can't come over after school today. I won't be riding the bus home. Mama's picking me up after school. I forgot to tell you," Julie says.

"Oh, well, that's all right. I was hoping we could spend the afternoon together picking out clothes for my trip or at least writing out a list of things I should take. Then I can see what else I need. You know there's still plenty of time to shop," Wendy replies.

"Always time to shop! If there's no time to shop, we make time to shop!" Julie says.

"Anyway, remind me to tell you at lunch. And nobody can sit by us. We'll sit in the corner alone so we can have some privacy. Okay?" Wendy asks.

"Okay. See, ya fourth period in social studies," Julie says.

As the two girls depart, Julie knows Wendy is disappointed but what can I do? I have my instructions from Mama. Wendy and I will get together another time and plan her wardrobe for Florida. However, Julie wonders. What is so important that Wendy needs us to sit alone? Julie thinks.

The day passes quickly. Too quickly! In math class, Mrs. Knight gives them a pop quiz. Not that Julie does badly, but she does not want another surprise. For some reason, surprises make me nervous. And I can't explain why, Julie thinks.

Julie notices that Nicole and Brittany are not at school. Those two sit in the back of the math class and they always know how to work the problems. Nicole especially sets the grading curve. Funny, Julie remembers that Nicole was not in school two days last week. As Julie thinks about it, Nicole misses school a lot. Julie wonders: how Nicole can miss so many days in school, keep up with all the math homework, and still get "A's" on every test?

When Julie goes to gym, she overhears some girls talking in the locker room.

"Did you hear about that man and his family on TV last night?" Sissy asks.

"Naw! I went to bed early. What happened?" Rachel asks.

"It seems as if this man was beating his wife and hit his daughter accidentally into a wall. Both the mother and daughter are badly injured. The daughter had emergency surgery last night. The mother is scheduled for surgery this morning. The news reporter said the daughter is in critical condition, while the mother is in fair condition," Sissy says.

"That's terrible," Rachel says.

"But that's not the end of it. The daughter might go to our school. We may even know her! The news reporter said the family lives in this area. The daughter is in seventh grade and goes to our school. The news reporter wouldn't say who the family is because the police asked him not to since the police are investigating a tip of where the father might be hiding. The father is still missing," Sissy says.

"I wonder: who could she be? Is there anybody who's in our class and not in school today?" Rachel asks.

"I know Nicole ain't been in school for a few days. And Brittany was absent yesterday and today. Anybody seen Brittany or Nicole?" Sissy asks. She gets responses from different girls in the gym class.

"Nope."

"Not, me."

"I haven't seen either one of them."

For the rest of the period, Julie wonders, is the news reporter even talking about someone at their school? He could have gotten the schools mixed up because there is another school eight blocks away. She thinks about how gossip travels and she wonders how she missed the news last night? Then Julie remembers Mama made her go to bed at 9 o'clock and turn out the lights at 10 o'clock. She must remember to ask Mama to let her watch the news more often. Julie does not want to be the only one, who does not know what is happening especially if it happens to someone in her school. Julie has other questions in her mind: "What is going on with Nicole and Brittany? Is the girl on the news either one of them? That would be awful!" Julie thinks.

In social studies, they are studying the family unit and family communications. As she arrives to her fourth period class, Julie thinks, "I wonder how Mama is? I hope she's all right. I..." But those thoughts are interrupted by yet another surprise as Mrs. Kent introduces her guest speaker from Social Services, Ms. Wimble. Julie looks behind her to get eye contact with Wendy. Wendy smiles, nods her head then scrunches up her nose. Widening her eyes, Julie smiles too. She is glad that Wendy is there. Wendy pulls out her notebook and pen.

Julie turns around in her seat to focus on what Ms. Wimble says because Mrs. Kent is known to give a pop quiz the next day to see, who paid attention the day before. Mrs. Kent passes out an outline to the class from Ms. Wimble.

[Here is the outline.]

Abuse: children/teenagers are hit or beaten. This is also called child abuse.

Child abuse happens when a parent, the father, mother or guardian hit the child inflicting bruises and wounds. Examples of child abuse are physical punching, slapping and discipline like a whipping done in anger, for no reason or for trivial reasons.

Examples of what abuse is not: Punishments like being on restriction for negative actions or a bad attitude for when a child/teenager cannot have their way.

Signs to recognize so that you can help somebody else:
1. Sometimes students have problems changing clothes in front of people because they have excessive scars that are unexplainable. Or the student may have an excuse like "I fell down the stairs."
2. Some students always wear dark glasses to cover up their black eyes, which happened because they say they bumped into a door. Or a student may say they accidentally hit their eye on something.

What to do if you suspect this is happening to someone you know:
1. Do not get paranoid. Sometimes these things do happen to students that are really accidents.
2. Talk with a teacher like Mrs. Kent. The teacher is able to investigate further if it is true and you will not have to get involved.
3. If you are not comfortable with talking with a teacher, maybe you feel better talking with the school counselor or the school nurse. They are trained to look into these things and you do not have to be involved.
4. If you are a student experiencing this, call our crisis hot line if you cannot call 911. The National Domestic Violence Hotline number is 1-800-799-7233. Someone will help you. There are people waiting to talk with you.

Julie took notes for herself.

class: social studies   date: February 25, 1999
speaker: Ms. Wimble from Social Services
subject: child abuse, domestic abuse

child abuse:
1. students have low self-esteam esteem (it affects their thinking).
2. students think it is their fault when this happens to them.

3. students only know this way of life and do not believe there is any other way to live.
4. students usually do not progress well in school or may progress extremely well to avoid ~~fyzical~~ physical punishment.
5. students usually have low school attendance.
6. students feel there is no way out. children are the victims.

domestic abuse

men hit wives -- just like my daddy and my mama ---- women hit husbands -Mama never hits Daddy. It's always been Daddy hitting Mama-- more often men hit their wives than women hit their husbands. legal in some countries, not the United States. called domestic violence. usually no one helps to stop it because it happens in the home between mothers and fathers. it happens to older adults like parents or grandparents living in the same homes as their children, grandchildren or other relatives.

reasons for domestic violence:
1. frustration
2. family history
3. anger or rage
4. person knows no other way of communicating

why it continues:
--it's difficult to deal with because
------the police are not notified
------sometimes if the police are called, no one ~~preses~~ presses charges...

At this point, Julie stops taking notes. The subject is painful and too much for her after all that happened the night before. She wonders: why is Mrs. Kent having Ms. Wimble come in and talk with us? Julie looks at what she wrote in her notes: *"just like my daddy and my mama... Mama* never hits Daddy. It's always been Daddy hitting Mama." Thinking about her own situation, she is confused. I love Daddy and Mama. Julie thinks.

But I also hate my daddy for hitting my mama and messing up our lives. But I cannot turn Daddy in! Maybe Mama would have been rescued by the police if I had called. What would have happened to me if I had called the police last night? How could I turn Daddy in like that? He never hits me: only Mama. What should I do? Should I call the police if it happens again? Julie thinks.

Wendy sits looking over her notes. *"Large dark glasses."* Ms. Wimble said. I remember so many times seeing Julie's mama with a huge scarf over her hair and large oversized sunglasses. Those sunglasses are so dark that you cannot see through them. And there was that one time when I saw a large bruise on Julie's mama's arm. Julie never explained what it was. Julie's mama said she bumped herself accidentally. Wendy thinks.

I wonder: is Julie's mama being abused? Maybe I should ask Julie? Mum bruises easily. So maybe I am being too suspicious. Father never hits Mum. I remember the time when Mum burned herself and had that nasty bruise for about three months. Perhaps all this is just a coincidence, considering the secret I have to tell Julie and all this talk about abuse from Ms. Wimble. Wendy thinks.

Julie blinks her eyes rapidly to fight back tears forming in her eyes. She feels she should not let anyone see her crying. Julie dares not look around at Wendy. It is at this point that she focuses again on what Ms. Wimble is saying.

Ms. Wimble explains that each case is different, which is why caution is used in each situation. Social Services have been able to help some families if they catch the case in enough time.

"I know this is a hard subject. But if any of you think you are being abused, do not hesitate to call our crisis hot line. If you don't want to call us: then talk with a teacher or a counselor. Whatever you do, (she pauses) please don't think it is your fault. It's happens. It's not your fault," Ms. Wimble says.

"And if one of your parents is hitt ng the other parent and you need to talk to someone, please give us a call. Or talk with a teacher or a counselor. (She pauses.) Let me tell you another reason why I'm here today. I'm here to talk with you about Nicole Gator. As you know, Nicole has been absent from school for almost a week. (She pauses.) Well... (She pauses.) Nicole won't be returning to school..." Ms. Wimble says. (She pauses again.)

Ms. Wimble looks into the eyes of the students in this class. She hates this part of her job. The last classroom she told this story to, a student had to be carried out. The girl was upset because she and Nicole had been good friends and were finally going to do something together this coming weekend. Now it is going to be impossible for the girl and Nicole to continue their friendship.

Ms. Wimble is surprised and grateful no one from that previous classroom is present now. The principal took some of those students into his office to let those students talk as long as they needed to. Ms. Wimble cannot take looking into the same hurt... shocked eyes twice. She reframes from shaking her head as she thinks: "The things students go through these days just to finish grammar school."

A murmur rolls through the classroom as Sissy whispers to Rachel, "I'll bet the girl on the news last night is Brittany or Nicole."

Slowly Ms. Wimble continues with her story.

"Well... there has been an accident with Nicole. She had emergency surgery last night."

Gasps ripple through the classroom.

"Nicole was that girl in the news last night, isn't she?" Sissy asks.

Ms. Wimble continues,

"Well... yes..." Ms. Wimble is interrupted.

"The news reported said she was in critical condition. She's gonna be all right, isn't she?" Sissy asks.

"We can go see her, right?" asks Brenise.

"No... you can't go see her in the hospital. Well... you see. (She pauses.) Nicole died early this morning... And... ah... (She pauses.) well..." Ms. Wimble says. (She pauses again.)

"Mrs. Gator passed about an hour later," Ms. Kent says quietly before Ms. Wimble can continue. Tears slowly trickle down Mrs. Kent's face.

The classroom is silent for a few minutes.

A few of the girl students break out in tears, sobbing loudly. Some of the boy students wipe their eyes and a few put their heads down so that no one will see them crying. Mrs. Kent walks through the classroom passing out facials tissues and leaving them on the corner of each desk. Tears roll down Julie's face. Wendy shakes her head in unbelief as her eyes filled with tears. A variety of outbursts from different classmates emit simultaneously.

"WHAT!"

"No way!"

"Not Nicole!"

"The news reporter said the father hurt his daughter!

Why would Mr. Gator hurt Nicole? I can't believe it! Why?" Sissy asks. Other students release more vocal outbursts.

"What a punk!"

"Are you sure it's Nicole Gator? Maybe it's a mistake!"

"Somebody ought to beat him up!"

Ms. Wimble explains that the news media agreed to withhold the names of the victims. With both Nicole and Mrs. Gator in the hospital, Mr. Gator had not been captured at the time. He ran before the police and the second ambulance arrived.

"The police traced Mr. Gator's whereabouts from his last phone call right after Nicole died. Apparently, he kept calling the hospital anonymously to check up on Nicole. They located him early this morning right before his wife died. Now that Mr. Gator has been captured, I'm sure the news reports are being released while we are in class," Ms. Wimble says softly. Changing her voice tone slightly, Ms. Wimble continues:

"I know this is hard." (Pausing again, she waits for a few minutes.)

"I understand... that Nicole was absent a lot. She covered up her body in gym class to camouflage scars or bruises on her body. She always wore tights. Occasionally, she wore large sunglasses or a patch over her eye to cover up a black eye. Nicole may have told you, she bumped her eye on a door, she had an eye problem or she said the glasses were her fashion statement. When in actuality, she possibly was being abused by one of her parents. A student in Nicole's previous classroom suspected something was wrong with Nicole. The student didn't say anything because she didn't want to get involved. It is highly probable this situation could have been avoided.

"We... don't (she pauses) want to see anything like that happen to any of you. (She pauses.) We would've liked to have helped Nicole. For Nicole, it's too late. But it's not too late for you. (She pauses.) We, at Social Services, don't want to separate children from their parents unless it's necessary. No one can help if nobody has any idea what is going on in your home. (She pauses again.) Let us help you. Get some help from somebody. Talk to somebody. Does anyone have any questions?" Ms. Wimble asks.

Heads shake back and forth signaling: "No" throughout the classroom. Julie sits there in shock. Wiping her eyes with a tissue, she thinks about this new development. **No! Not Nicole! Not Mrs. Gator!** She was so nice. **Nicole is gone!** She was one of my good friends. Julie shakes her head in unbelief. She will no longer be able to see Nicole's bright smile again.

What about my situation? Should I talk with someone? Julie stares at the 800 number. Should I call it? Julie thinks. Just then, the bell rings to go to fifth period. Mr. Stevens, the assistant principal stands in the doorway with Mr. Evans, the school counselor.

It is lunch time for Julie and Wendy.

"Oh, one other thing before you leave," comments Mrs. Kent with tears running down her face.

"If you need to talk with anyone, I'm here for you. (She pauses.) If you need to talk with someone right now, you can go immediately to the principal's office and someone is waiting to talk with you. Mr. Evans will escort you. (She pauses and sighs.) If you miss your next class, it'll be all right. You are excused if you're in the principal's office. Thank you, Ms. Wimble for coming today," Mrs. Kent says. Her voice quakes a little and she reaches for a facial tissue to blow her nose. Half of the classmates leave and the other half sit in their seats for a few minutes.

Wendy sits at her seat trembling, wiping away her tears and praying.

"God, how did this happen? I don't understand! How could somebody kill their own daughter?"

Wendy thinks for a moment: "What if that had been Julie, not Nicole and Julie had died? How would I feel losing my best friend like that?" Wendy does not feel like eating lunch at this time. But she needs to talk this through with a friend, her best friend: Julie.

Julie does not really feel like lunch today. She thinks about her parents. "Mama may be in trouble or real danger! My parents may need some help. Perhaps Social Services can help them. Ms. Wimble said Social Services cannot help the children if they, Social Services, do not know about their situation."

Standing up, Julie gathers her books, notes and tissue. She throws her tissue in the garbage can, smiles at Mrs. Kent and Ms. Wimble and walks toward the door. Turning around, Julie watches Mrs. Kent and Ms. Wimble. They are trying to console Brenise, who is not only crying but stuttering and shaking. While the two women attempt to get Brenise to calm down, Grace bends her head forward on her desk and moans uncontrollably. Mrs. Kent leaves Ms. Wimble with Brenise and runs to Grace. Grace and Nicole were best friends.

"Not Nicole! I tried to call her. (She sobs.) She wouldn't return my phone calls! I didn't know she had an accident. (She sobs.) Maybe I could've gone to see her last night in the hospital. Mom would've taken me. Nicole didn't even tell me what was happening to her. **MAYBE, I**

COULD'VE TOLD SOMEBODY. I COULD'VE..." Grace shouts. (She stops.)

"Grace, it's okay to be upset. It's okay, honey," Mrs. Kent says placing her arm around Grace. Mrs. Kent lifts Grace from her seat and allows Grace to crumple into her arms.

Danny, who is on the other side of Grace, just sits there. I had a secret crush on Nicole and now she's dead. Nicole is gone forever. She is not coming back just like Grandfather, who died three weeks ago, Danny thinks.

The more Danny thinks about his grandfather, the more tears flow down his face. Then Danny's thoughts return to Nicole again. He tries wiping his eyes to stop the tears but he cannot stop tears from flowing down his face.

Mr. Stevens walks quietly over to Danny and puts a strong hand on Danny's shoulder. Why did he do that? "It reminds me of the way Grandfather used to just walk over and place a strong hand on my shoulder." Danny thinks. Danny breaks into loud sobs.

"Son, it's all right to cry," Mr. Stevens says. "I know it hurts. Nicole must've been a good friend."

"It's... it's... not just Nicole! I... I... (he sobs) her dying... reminds me... of my grandfather... My grandfather died three weeks ago! I I..." Danny says. He stops talking unable to explain further.

Mr. Stevens raises Danny from his seat, wraps his arms around Danny and hugs him real tight. He remembers he was about Danny's age when his grandfather died. Mr. Stevens also remembers that no matter, who died after that, it took Mr. Stevens a long time to stop crying because it hurt so much.

As Mrs. Kent holds Grace and allows her to cry in her

bosom, she focuses on Julie. Julie is just standing there in the doorway watching the whole situation with a strange look on her face. It is almost as if Julie 's not there.

"Julie, are you all right?" Mrs. Kent questions.

Julie looks directly at Mrs. Kent and nods her head. Then Julie slowly walks out of the room. She has to have time to think. The noise in the hallway of students passing between classes does not help. Lockers clang and students laugh loudly right outside of the room. It's hard but Julie tries to focus on what to do.

Thinking about what Ms. Wimble said. Julie comes to her own conclusions: Nicole nor Ms. Gator would not have died if they weren't at home for Mr. Gator to hit them. It's too late for them but not for Mama. What if Mama leaves Daddy? If Mama's not at home, Daddy can't hit her. If Daddy doesn't hit Mama 'cause Mama isn't there then Mama will live and not die. I've got to talk with Mama! She must leave Daddy so she lives. I don't want my mama to be dead like Mrs. Gator, Julie thinks.

Just then, Wendy catches up with Julie. Wendy has been trailing behind Julie for a little while.

"Julie, are you okay? Julie... Julie... answer me!" Wendy says loudly.

Julie turns and focuses on Wendy for a moment. She wonders: how long has Wendy been following me and talking? Julie forgot all about Wendy and left Wendy in the classroom. Usually, they walk out together. The second bell rings signaling the start of the fifth period.

"Oh, Wen, girl, I've just had too many surprises today. I don't know if I can take another one," Julie says. Tears form in her eyes then flow down her face.

"Julie, we're going into the restroom so you and I both

can calm down. I'm so upset," says Wendy. She steers Julie through the restroom doors.

"This is the secret I had to tell you. I knew that Nicole's family was having problems at home because I heard Mum praying last night with Sister Loretta from church. Mum and Sister Loretta prayed that Mrs. Gator would leave and not stay until things changed with Mr. Gator. Mrs. Gator came to church for counseling and was scared to go home earlier this week. I was hoping you and I could pray for Nicole or maybe even get Nicole to talk about what was going on at home. But now that's impossible!" Wendy says.

"Now, she's dead! I don't know what went wrong? I've been praying and asking God: what happened??? How could this happen to somebody we know?" Wendy says in a shaky voice.

"I know. I only thought it happened in the movies or on TV. And especially not to Nicole! She was such a nice person. Oh, Wen, girl, I still can't believe it happened! We need to pray together. There is strength when more than one person prays. You go ahead and pray," Julie says.

Wendy prays:

"Lord, Daddy God I don't know why this happened to Nicole. But you do. Please help my friend, Julie and me to calm down. We need your help and your peace right now. Please, help us to understand, in Jesus' name, Amen."

Wendy reaches into her book bag and gets her Bible.

Julie looks at Wendy after she has prayed. Wendy is really a good friend. A person I can trust, Julie thinks. And the prayer must have worked because I feel calmer now and a peace coming over me. Wiping her eyes, Julie walks over to the face bowl and splashes cold water on her face. Taking a deep breath, she sighs and looks at Wendy again. What would I do without a friend like Wendy? Julie thinks about her home situation. She is not ready to share her secret with Wendy just yet.

Julie thinks again about her Mama. The thought comes back to her again: what if Mama had d ed like Ms. Gator? I have to say something. Maybe Wendy can keep this secret and only pray with me? God hears the prayers of kids. God heard that little girl, who worked for Naaman's wife. God heard Miriam, Moses' sister and David's prayers. But David was a teenager. He does not count. God did hear Miriam's prayers and that other little girl's prayers, who worked for Naaman's wife.

God also heard Wendy and my prayers when we prayed for other kids here at school. God heard Wendy's prayer a moment ago. Maybe God will hear us if we pray for Mama, Julie thinks.

Wendy finishes praying and looks at Julie again. Julie wipes the water from her face. Julie looks as if she is not here but far far away. Maybe Julie is thinking about all the surprises that have happened. Wendy cannot believe it herself that Nicole is dead. It is as if we're in some bad dream together that will not go away. Not just Nicole is gone, but Ms. Gator is gone too. This is awful. How many more surprises in this day will happen? Flipping through her bible, there has got to be a scripture here we can use now, Wendy thinks. As Wendy thinks about what to say next and looks for a scripture, Julie speaks.

"Wen, I have a secret to tell you. But you must promise me that you won't tell anyone even your mum. I'll only tell you if you promise me that Wen," Julie says. Julie looks very sober as if this is a dreaded thing, Wendy thinks.

"You're my girl, Julie. If you want me to keep it secret and not tell Mum, it won't be the first time. It's okay. I promise I won't tell anyone especially Mum. You can count on me," Wendy says. Julie takes a deep breath and speaks.

"Okay, well this is it... This is my secret. Don't tell your mum. Well... here it is. Daddy hits Mama. He did it again last night. He never hits me because I hide. Mama told me always to hide and pray when Daddy is so angry that he starts yelling then hitting her. I lock the doors: the door to my bedroom and the closet door. I hide, pray and sing. And I ask God: why is this happening to Mama?

"I don't come out until Mama comes to get me and tells me it's okay to come out. Sometimes I end up sleeping in the closet because Daddy yells and hits Mama into the early morning hours. Please... please don't tell your mum. This morning was different. Mama looked really bad. One of her eyes is almost swollen shut and there is blood everywhere. I'm so scared that my mama may not make it one day just like Ms. Gator. I was thinking Mama should leave Daddy. Ms. Wimble said it was too late for Nicole and Mrs. Gator but not for anyone else. It's not too late for my mama. If Mama is not home then Daddy can't hit her," Julie says.

Wendy stands there looking at Julie with a blank stare on her face. Julie has tears streaming down her cheeks. Wendy cannot believe what she is hearing. Here is another surprise! **Julie's daddy hits her mama!** Wendy gets flash backs in her mind of all the times Julie's mama wore those huge dark sunglasses, long sleeves, and an oversized head scarf even when it was hot outside. I have to think now. I can't lose another friend to this thing of the enemy. I won't lose Julie this way, Wendy says to herself.

Then almost impulsively Wendy hugs Julie and they both cry. A fifth grade girl walks into the restroom with a restroom pass and stares at them strangely. They step apart with tears flowing down both of their faces. They go to the sinks and splash water on their faces. Then they both wipe their faces and sit on the floor quietly waiting for the girl to finish in the restroom and wash her hands. She finishes. She washes her hands and looks at them then rapidly leaves the restroom murmuring to herself that the seventh graders are acting strange again. The girl's comments make the two of them burst into hearty laughter.

Both of them diminished laughing and Wendy takes a deep breath.

"Julie have you talked with your mama about leaving? We just lost Nicole. Oh my God! I don't want to lose you too," Wendy says.

"I just thought about it today after hearing what happened to Nicole as I was walking in the hallway," Julie says.

"Wen I don't even know if Mama will leave Daddy?" Julie continues.

"And I don't know what to do? I've been asking God to make Daddy stop but Daddy still does it. I don't want my mama to die. If Mama is not at our house then Daddy can't hit her.

"Oh Wen girl, pray with me that Mama agrees to leave Daddy. If Mama is not home then Daddy can't hit her. I don't want Mama to end up like Ms. Gator. And I don't think Daddy would hit me but who knows? Nobody thinks a father will hit a daughter and the daughter dies!!! I don't want to end up like Nicole. Besides, if we leave, where would we live? I may never see you again," Julie says sadly.

Wendy looks Julie straight in her eyes.

"Girl, don't worry about where you'll live. I don't want you to leave either but at least you'll be alive. We know God. He will find a way for you and me to connect. I don't know where or how but some kind of way we'll see each other again. Yes, I'll pray with you and talk to God about it since I can't tell anybody else," Wendy says.

Julie smiles at Wendy. Maybe if we ask God, He will make Mama see it is important for her to leave Daddy so that she can live. Prayer is good. Maybe Mama will listen to God especially after I tell her about Nicole and Mrs. Gator. Maybe that will make Mama leave Daddy, Julie thinks.

"I want to start the prayer this time, have you agree with me and you finish it," Julie says out loud.

"I was just thinking. Maybe Mama will listen to God about leaving Daddy after we pray and I tell her about Nicole and Mrs. Gator," Julie says.

The two girls hold each other's hands as they sit on the floor. Julie prays.

"Father God it's us again today. We know you love us and our parents. We ask you in the name of Jesus to heal Mama. Please let there be no damage to her eye and the rest of her body.

"Father God please let her live and not die. Can you talk with Mama and tell her to leave Daddy so that we don't get killed like Nicole and Mrs. Gator. I don't want us to die too. Please show Mama where to go and how to get there."

Julie pauses for a moment and Wendy continues the prayer.

"Daddy God I agree with this prayer. If Julie leaves with her mama, I'm going to miss her but I would rather she be alive somewhere else than dead in her house. Please see that we connect some kind of way somewhere and keep them safe and alive in Jesus name amen," Wendy says.

"Amen. Thank you. I feel better and God always comes through," Julie says.

Julie releases Wendy's hands and hugs her right then. Wendy is a good friend that I can trust with my secret. I'm glad I finally told somebody. I'm glad it's Wen. This may be the only way Daddy will stop hitting Mama. Maybe this is God's way of answering all those prayers I prayed for Daddy to stop hitting Mama. Besides, if Mama is not in the house then Daddy can't hit her, Julie thinks.

Wendy hugs Julie one more time. This might be the last time we get to talk like this and be together. We have been through so much. Why I've known Julie since we were 3 years old. Now we're 12 years old and in seventh grade together. What will life be without Julie to talk to and laugh with? Wendy thinks.

"You know girl, you got my digits," Wendy says out loud breaking the silence.

"We can keep in touch like that if you can call from wherever you are if your mama decides to leave and you go with her," Wendy says.

Both girls laugh.

"Yeah, you're right. I have your telephone number. Maybe your mum will let us talk on the phone if I'm not around," Julie says smiling.

The bell rings and lunch time is over. The two girls get

up off the floor, dust their clothes off and exit the restroom. As they go to their respective classes, they say "bye." Each hoping this is not the last time they will be together but knowing deep down inside that it may be the last time as ***God always answers their prayers whenever they pray together***.

Three

Years

Later

Chapter 5
A Second Chance

The sun shines brightly through the curtains of the windows of their apartment. Looking out the windows, she focuses on the ground. No more snow, that's good, Elizabeth thinks. She gets on her knees and prays. As Elizabeth prays, tears roll down her cheeks.

"Father God, I thank you for waking me up this morning. I thank you for my new life without Julio. Thank you for a second chance at love, friends and family. I thank you for healing me and letting me live. That I only stayed in the hospital for four days and you gave me someone, who took special care of my daughter while I was there. I thank you that a grant covered my hospital expenses. I thank you for the peace and quiet in this home. God, I thank you for a place where I never thought I would ever be or would ever have: a free woman with a job outside of her home.

"I thank you for Julie and me living in this new place where we don't have to run anymore. I thank you I no longer live in fear of Julio beating me. You did not give us fear and fear doesn't live in my house any more. Thank you Jesus!

"Thank you for the wisdom to change our names legally as a protective measure after the divorce was final. I like Elizabeth for me instead of Pam. It's like being a famous person with a private name. I thank you I agreed to have those pictures taken that last time Julio beat me. Those pictures helped me to see my situation and gave me favor with the judge in court. The judge gave me complete custody of Julie.

"I know you hate divorce and I ask you to forgive me again. Yet I also know that neither you, God nor Jesus beats the person you love. I thank you Father God for letting Julie visit her abuela (Spanish for grandmother) only three times a year as a condition of the divorce order. Thank you that my brother, Big Dee agreed to take her and stay with her so that she remains safe.

"God I love you and appreciate you. Daddy God, I thank you for my new mind and my new self-esteem. I know that I am valuable just as I am because you made me this way and You don't make junk! I am not junk! Thank you God I have learned so much these past three years. Let me be able to give donations to other domestic violence shelters to help someone else. Show me how or where to get the money for it.

"Help me to remember to call Julie: Rosita. Bless Rosita and me today with your favor. Help Rosita complete all her assignments in school and get 'A's.' Keep her safe going to and from school. I send angels to be with her and me as we travel. Help me to finish my work in excellence, in Jesus name amen."

When she finishes praying, Elizabeth glances at the clock. She still has half an hour before she has to wake up

Rosita. Rosita is a good new name for Julie. It mixes both cultures: her black heritage and Julio's Hispanic heritage. Moreover, Rosita is a natural name for Julie. Now if I only can remember to call Julie Rosita instead of Julie all things would be good, Elizabeth thinks.

So many changes have occurred in three short years. The day that seemed like the day of hell, turned out to be a turning point of blessing in my life, Elizabeth thinks. After we registered in the shelter, I received hospital care, prayer, counseling and help. I got divorced. We changed our names. I went back to school to finish my college degree. I only had a year to go and I completed that in nine months. Imagine me as old as I am finishing college. Smiling again, I wasn't the oldest student there either. There were four other students older than me.

Then I got this wonderful job offer here in Chicago. It is so far away from Julio and his family. We found a new church home. I can't visit them like I desire because Julio still lives in that city. Yet I still have great friends in Sister Cindy: Wendy's mom, Sister Sheri, Sister Toni, Sister Irene, Sister Desiree and my newest friend, Sister Sita from the first shelter we stayed at in Willow County, Elizabeth thinks.

I'm glad I changed our names. That time Julio came looking for us and almost found us at the first shelter where we stayed at was enough for me to change our names legally. I'm also glad we changed our names in a different county, one of the largest counties in Illinois. This way Julio will have a difficult time finding our new names because we are not in a county close by. And we got used to them in each new location we moved to.

We had just moved the day before to a new shelter

because that one was the most likely one for him to find us at since it was so close to our town. Sister Sita, my friend at the first shelter, who worked at the same place I did temporarily; told me Julio was questioning the director the very next day after we moved! Sister Sita said Julio shouted at the director that she could not keep him from his wife and child, Elizabeth thinks.

When Julio couldn't get the information he wanted, he told the director he would be back with the police. Leaving in a rage, Julio kicked the tires on his car before he got into it. About two days later Julio brought the police back. It was to no avail because the director had no idea which shelter we moved to. So all the director could say legally was: we left.

Julio is not the first husband or boyfriend to follow someone to that shelter. I'm glad we listened to the director when she told us it was time to move to a different shelter. And I'm glad she did not desire to know which one. The director gave us a list of shelters to choose from. So that when we moved, she did not know for sure which location we moved to. Elizabeth thinks.

We survived the 1999 Y2K scare that everything would freeze up, which had electronic devices operating them. I could not believe that some churches agreed with that prediction about 12/31/1999 at 11:59 p.m.! Were they not hearing from God? God didn't tell me anything. We were advised to prepare for Y2K whatever way we could by everyone else.

Y2K for the new Millennium was that on 1/1/2000 precisely at 12:00 a.m.: we would have no water, no money, no food and no movement at all because of all the electronic chips or devices, previously installed years earlier.

And regardless of where they were installed commercially, industrially or personally when time rolled over into that minute none of them would work. According to the experts, there was no provision on any of the electronic chips or mechanisms to handle moving into that precise minute and date of 01/01/2000. Elizabeth thinks.

Some people took all their money out of their accounts. Slowly, I accepted the belief myself. Since I wasn't sure what to believe I removed all my money out of my bank accounts on 12/31/1999 right before the banks closed. I took that money home. Then to make sure I had water to flush my toilet after midnight and wash my body with, I filled the bathtub with water and purchased lots of water in plastic gallon containers from the store. Not only did my car work but nothing happened with my bank accounts either. I put all that money back in my bank accounts on 1/2/2000, when the banks opened after the holiday. I let the water out of the tub and drank those gallons of water one by one. That was something. God, you are good! You knew all along nothing would happen.

Then there was the United States of America's catastrophe on 9/11/2001 (9/11/01) that everyone calls today the "911 Tragedy." Terrorists hijacked four airplanes with passengers on them. The first plane hit the north tower of the World Trade Center in heart of New York City before 9 a.m. Glass, concrete, dust and building materials were everywhere. The impact was heard and seen for miles from that area. Immediately, New York's Policemen and Firemen were on the scene. New York City's Emergency Command Center was on the 23rd floor adjacent to the Twin Towers (the north and south buildings). Elizabeth thinks.

I remember reading the rest of the explicit details on

the Internet of what happened since I'm in Chicago and only saw what they put on the news. Less than 20 minutes later a second plane smashed the south tower of the World Trade Center. I saw the footage on TV of that second impact because the media was on site reporting to the world. Wow that was really scary!

Firemen and police were already on the scene evacuating people inside one of the twin towers because of that north tower's hit. The south tower crumbled in less than an hour! Almost half hour later after the south tower fell, the north tower collapsed. People were not completely evacuated. The people, who were in the process of leaving the building and those rescuing people, were trapped inside when the building crumbled. It was horrible! Today, the Twin Towers, which were iconic to New York City, are completely gone! Elizabeth thinks.

The four surrounding World Trade Buildings: Four, Five, Six and Seven were on fire. Nine hours later World Trade Building Seven, which housed the New York City Emergency Command Center collapsed completely. All the people in World Trade Building Seven where the command center was, had been evacuated already when it first caught fire.

The third plane hit the Pentagon in Washington, D.C. killing many people employed by the military. The fourth plane crashed in a field in Pennsylvania. Firemen and policemen from around the United States came to assist in all four disaster areas, Elizabeth thinks.

Just think I almost took that prestigious position at the World Trade Center for that stock exchange company as an administrative assistant to the vice president of that division! That job was so tempting. I would have made three times the amount money I make now with a company car, my own parking space and a company expense account. I don't even know if that company still exists or if the vice president of that company is alive. I'm so glad I did not take it. Julie... I mean Rosita might have been without a mother if I had worked there! Then she may have had to go live with Julio. Ugh! Elizabeth thinks.

Deep in thoughts of thankfulness and counting her blessings, the clock startles Elizabeth ringing at 5:30 a.m. Jumping out of bed, she heads for Rosita's room. Opening the door and glancing at her daughter, who has finally grown as tall as Wendy used to be over her, she smiles once again.

Rosita has her arm wrapped around her favorite red and black stuffed animal. Some things never change. I think this one may sleep with her favorite red and black stuffed animal until she gets married, Elizabeth thinks.

"Julie... I mean Rosita it's time to get up for school. Say your prayers while I get a shower. Rosita... you hear me calling you, get up now. And let your favorite stuffed animal's head go. You might give him a headache," Elizabeth says laughing.

"Oh, Mama he's okay. I need to go to the restroom before I pray," Rosita says.

"Go ahead and I'll put some meat in the oven for breakfast," Elizabeth says. Rosita goes to the restroom, washes her hands, goes back to her bedroom, kneels down and says her morning prayers.

After washing her hands, turning on the oven, putting the meat in the oven and heading for the bathroom, Elizabeth looks in Rosita's room one more time to make sure she hasn't gone back to sleep. Good, she didn't. Rosita is on her knees praying. Walking into the bathroom and before she closes the door to wash her body, Elizabeth says,

"I can't take you to school today because I have to go to a meeting. So whatever you wear, put on layers. You'll have to take the bus today. It is warmer outside this morning but the temperature is supposed to drop again this afternoon."

"Aw, no ride today! It's still cold outside," Rosita says. Grabbing her favorite stuffed animal by his neck, Rosita looks him in the eyes and says,

"Would your mama do you like this, make you catch the bus to school when it's cold outside? Oh yeah that right you don't talk. I guess I'll have to talk to Father God or Jesus about it instead. They both answer prayer and talk back. It's time to finish my prayers and thank God for our new home and that Mama is alive."

Both mother and daughter shower, get dressed, eat breakfast and leave the apartment. They get into the car to go to their respective destinations. Elizabeth drops Rosita at the bus stop three blocks away.

Chapter 6
Lost in Thoughts

The bus fills up quickly with students trying to get to their respective schools on time or early. At each bus stop, the bus becomes a little bit more crowded. Finally it takes a lot of time to unload and load people. It takes even more time when the bus driver has to tell people to let the other people off the bus first before boarding the bus. Some people do not honor this standard protocol of bus operation.

Some adults look angry as more and more high school students pile into the bus. Some high school students stand over adults holding onto the bus hand straps while other students squeeze into whatever space they can fit in. A few students give up their seats to the older people, especially those with white or gray hair. Other students discuss loudly what was on the news and television the night before. There are so many students on the bus that the bus driver drives express and passes several potential passengers for the last five stops before they arrive at Rosita's school because there is no more room on the bus for anyone else.

Stepping off the bus, Rosita Lee heads toward the school building. Finally! It is a warmer day in Chicago with no snow on the ground. Rosita wears her red lined, patent leather boots with her red pants, matching red coat, red mittens, red hat and red scarf. Her blouse is white with red trim on the edges and ends of her short sleeves. She has on a red wool sweater over her blouse because Mama said she had to layer to stay warm today. Rosita's new friends and classmates always tease her because her favorite color was and is still red.

Looking down quickly at her designer watch, Rosita glances at the time. Walking rapidly, she realizes that she must hurry if she wants to get to class on time. Rosita is glad she ate before she left home and has a few snacks in her back pack.

Though it is warmer, it isn't 60° outside just 40°! Students are conversing everywhere. Climbing the steps to the building, Rosita enters in. Rosita's locker partner waits with their locker opened so they can go to honors biology together. She heads to her locker to unload some of her books and she puts her mittens inside her hat in her locker. Rosita hangs her coat on a hook and keeps her sweater on as her first class tends to be a bit chilly even when the heat in the building is turned up.

"Girl, you made it just in time. What took you so long to get here today?" Shawn asks.

"I didn't get a ride to school from my older brother just like you did, Ms. Shawn," Rosita says.

"And you know what took so long... 'the big green bus!!!' Mama couldn't drop me at school today 'cause she had a meeting downtown she had to get to. So I rode the big green bus today. There were so many students that the driver drove express for the last six or seven... well maybe at least the last five stops to get here. The bus rises up higher after all our high school students get off. Some older people were glad 'cause I saw a few running for our empty seats," says Rosita.

"Those people are tired even before they get to work," says Shawn. Rosita lightens her back pack load by removing books she will not need for the next three periods. Picking up her biology lab book, stuffing it into her red back pack, she turns to Shawn and asks,

"You finished here?"

"Yeah, I got everything for now. You ready?" Shawn asks.

"Yep as much as possible, I hope we don't have a pop quiz the first thing this morning. I don't like them even though I studied just in case," Rosita says.

"Girl and you know it! I'm glad we're locker partners and have honors biology together," Shawn says.

"Yep, you my girl too! We'd better hurry. I don't want any points taken off for being late to class," Rosita says. Rosita closes their locker and locks it. She and Shawn talk as they walk to class.

"I know I came from a small town but do you ever get use to all the students in the hallways?" Rosita asks Shawn.

"Aw girl this ain't nothing. My cousin goes to Naperville North High School in the suburbs and they have three times as many students as we do," says Shawn.

"'Cuse us, please," Shawn says to the group of students standing in the middle of the hallway two classrooms down from where they have to go.

"Three times as many students in a high school, that's crazy," Rosita says as they enter their class.

Taking their seats, the bell rings. Looking at each other they smile. Just in time they both think. Mr. Williams starts to close the door. Anyone entering the class once the door is closed is considered late and points are taken off their attendance. As he is pulling the door closed; Earl, Jerred and Brina shoot in the room through the door ducking under Mr. Williams' arm. He gives them a scouring look and pulls the door shut. They made it by the skin of their teeth, Rosita thinks.

Four more students trickle in after the door is shut:

Percy, Elizabeth, Francine and Preston. Rosita saw them standing outside on that first bus stop the bus driver passed up. They were waiting for the next green bus. Each student stops by Mr. Williams and explains to him why they are late before they can sit down. It is his decision to let them stay in class. He accepts their excuses and lets them sit down.

I'm here for two periods today because it is a lab day. We discussed dissecting the frog last week and my lab partner is Percy. I'm glad he made it here as it is the second week of classes. Percy is a medium weight, round guy. He only comes up to my nose in height. He isn't tall enough to be my type at all. Rosita thinks.

Rosita writes down in her notebook the homework assignment already written on the board. She doesn't desire to try to call anybody about it. She wants to have it written for herself in her own notebook so there is no misunderstanding about what she has to do.

While Mr. Williams takes attendance, Rosita begins to day dream a bit before class officially starts. I like my high school. I'm a sophomore with all honor classes except Spanish, gym and art. I really like my Spanish class with my Spanish teacher, who lived in Ciudad Guzman, Mexico for a short time. What I like most is: not having to fear that maybe Mama might end up dead from Daddy hitting her. God is so good! He answered my prayers and Daddy can't hit Mama because we don't live with him anymore. Rosita thinks.

I'm glad Mama lets me talk with Wendy every now and then. I couldn't at first since Daddy kept showing up at Wendy's house asking Mrs. Whitlow, Wendy's mum: where were we? They didn't know 'cause Mama wouldn't let me tell

Wendy. Then Mrs. Whitlow told me I couldn't call for about five months so that Wendy would not be lying to Daddy when she said she had not talked with me. I'm sorry that Mrs. Whitlow had to have the police stop Daddy from coming by their house and stopping by school to ask Wendy questions.

Now that Mama and Daddy's divorce is final, maybe I'll get to visit Wendy one day after I visit my abuela. I'm glad my uncle Dee goes with me to see my abuela. Daddy showed up that one time before the divorce was final. He scared me really bad demanding to know: where was Mama? I was crying and shaking. Uncle Dee called the police on his big black cellular phone from his job clipped to his belt. The police made Daddy leave. My abuela apologized and said she didn't know that Daddy was going to scare me like that or ask questions about Mama. Abuela promised me that she would not tell Daddy the next time I was coming to visit her and would call Uncle Dee if Daddy showed up unannounced. Rosita thinks.

Lost in her thoughts, Rosita does not hear Mr. Williams asking her a question nor realize he is standing right in front of her with someone standing behind him. The whole lab class giggles. Looking up and embarrassed, Rosita apologizes and asks Mr. Williams what is the question he just asked her?

"I asked you Rosita if for the rest of the day you would show around our newest student, Wendy, who just transferred to our school? I checked your schedule and you two both have the exact same classes. This way she can learn where everything is," says Mr. Williams.

Rosita thinks: really! Now there's another person named Wendy? Looking past Mr. Williams, Rosita stares right into the face of her friend: Wendy in a coal black bobbed haircut. She is wearing brown corduroy pants, a cream long sleeved sweater, and brown knee-length leather boots. Rosita doesn't know what to say. Wendy looks a bit shocked by Julie answering to Rosita because she immediately recognizes Rosita as Julie even though Julie's hair color is coal black like hers. Wendy just winks her eye at Rosita.

"Well, Ms. Rosita we don't have all day! We have a lab to do. Will you do it?" Mr. Williams asks. The class smirks a little this time and giggles flow through the room. Mr. Williams turns around and glares at them. The class settles down from slightly noisy to quiet.

"Yeah, sure," says Rosita.

"Good, that's settled. Wendy for today only: you'll sit with Rosita and Percy during this lab. By Thursday, I'll have you your own lab partner. Is that okay with you?" asks Mr. Williams.

"Yes," Wendy says. Raising his voice, Mr. Williams says,

"Okay then everyone pickup your sheets for this lab and your dissecting tools. Go to your stations with your lab partner or partners, put on your gloves and began dissecting your specimen. Make sure you label all the appropriate systems located on the specimen and the lab sheet as we'll have a quiz this Thursday at your next lab of what you did today. Is that clear?" asks Mr. Williams.

The lab class grumbles in various voices "Yeah" instead of yes and Mr. Williams gets the point. Rosita cannot believe it! Right next to her is her best friend, Wendy!

I was just thinking about her! Wendy has a great haircut. And today we're going to be lab partners here in Chicago at my high school! How cool is that God? But will

Wendy keep my secret? All the students and teachers know me as Rosita not Julie. I finally got comfortable with being called Rosita by them and that took a long time for me, thinks Rosita.

I can't believe it God! I'm here with my best friend that I have not seen in three years! I wonder: are we still best friends? I kept my mouth shut because I almost shouted out: Julie! I was surprised to hear Mr. Williams call Julie Rosita and not Julie. She never said anything on the phone the last time we talked that her name is changed. God I'm glad I didn't give her secret away. But will we be able to be friends like we were in the past? I'm different now. Wendy thinks.

I've been through so much. Mr. Perez, Julie's father following me and harassing me when Julie and Mrs. Perez left him. We had to get the police to stop him. Father almost died from a heart attack. He had emergency surgery here in Chicago when he was here on a business trip. Mum went to work when I started eighth grade. I wasn't used to that. I had more chores to do to help around the house. I made my own lunches. I started dinner every night or cooked it completely for Mum when I got home from school. Plus I did my homework.

Next, we moved here to Chicago for better doctors, hospitals, schools and better jobs: both Mum's and Father's. We moved into a great house in this new neighborhood. But I don't know those people. It's so cold here that I haven't got to know anyone. I saw this cute guy on the block but it's too cold to sit outside so he can notice me. I miss Jerry. We became best friends after Julie left. We talked all the time. Now we are too far away to be boyfriend and girlfriend. I've got to find a new boyfriend,

Wendy thinks.

I'm tired of looking at Rosita in her different red outfits almost every other day. She always wears some kind of red. That is my cousin, Antwan's favorite color. Rosita can be bossy when we work on our projects. But "look a here... look a here," this here Wendy is fine! I like this brown outfit. It's cute. Look at her coal black hair, straight with just a little curl at the end. Now that's what I'm talking about! My favorite color on her and she is tall and fine! Percy thinks.

Rosita looks at both Percy and Wendy. Percy has a strange smile on his face and is staring dreamingly at Wendy. Wendy has a glazed look on her face. Both of them look like they are far far away lost in their own thoughts. The two of them daydreaming and nothing is written on either of their sheets. We have to complete this work before the end of the period, Rosita thinks. Rosita takes action.

"Percy and... ah... Wendy is it? Do you guys have anything written down? We have to finish our work in the next 30 minutes. Here's what I have so far on my sheet. I'll share so you can finish," Rosita says.

Percy and Wendy snap out of their trances and begin writing. They finish as the bell rings for the third period. Packing up and zipping up their book bags, the three leave the lab heading to their next class.

Rosita whispers to Wendy,

"Thanks for keeping my secret." Wendy smiles at Julie.

12 Years Later

Chapter 7
The Look

Bobbing her head to the beat of her old school c.d., Julie guides her car by the steering wheel to the left as she turns unto Ogden Ave. She heads toward her apartment. The hot wind blows through her car causing her swooped up braided black curls to move around. She presses buttons to close all the windows, snaps close the hood and turns the air conditioning on. Julie thinks to herself, although my hair is naturally curly I do not want my braided curled hair to lose the definition of its curls this early in the evening.

Turning again onto Cherry Street, she stops in front of 212 SE Cherry Street, which is where she and Wendy live. Honking the horn, Julie parks her black 1999 car in front of their apartment complex: Eagle's Ricge. Looking up, Julie smiles as she acknowledges Wendy's wave from their balcony. Their apartment is on the third floor. Julie just returned from getting film at the local drugstore, which carries toiletries, groceries, film and pharmaceutical items.

Glancing into the mirror above the steering wheel on the driver's side, Julie checks her makeup one last time and smiles at the sunlight bouncing off her looped 14k gold earrings. She is glad she made that purchase. It was a wise investment. Besides, these days gold is becoming scarce and platinum is becoming more popular. Simple yellow gold is enough for her. Julie got this trait from her abuela.

Rewinding the c.d., she has to admit after all these years she still likes this c.d. best. Julie's friends are forever trying to get her come out of the 1990's and enter into the

21st century, which is a new millennium. Although Julie likes this gospel artist's newest c.d., there is something about this c.d. that is special to her. Maybe it's the fact that her favorite song, "Lean on Me," is on it. Julie presses the buttons to unlock the doors as Wendy approaches the car.

Wendy's long pearl drop earrings sparkle and glisten as does the necklace on her freckled neck. The pearls she wears match the stitched-on pearls surrounding her red-satin jacket and dress. Wendy opens the front door on the passenger side of the car and slides in. Grabbing the seat belt on her right, pulling to her left and smoothing out her floor-length, red-satin dress, Wendy fastens it in place across her waist. She holds her gold purse that matches her gold 4" heels.

"I got the film. You ready to go?" Julie asks.

"Yes, what took you so long? The drugstore is only five minutes away. You should have been back a little while ago," Wendy says.

"Oh, there was some old lady ahead of me in line paying with cash instead of tokens. You know how that can take up time because the young clerk didn't know how to count without the computer. When the clerk finally finished that transaction, it took her a while to locate the 7000 speed film, which fits both of our cameras. It was on the shelf right behind her head. Since she was the only person at the drive up window, it took more time to finish our transaction even though I handed her tokens for her computer," Julie replies.

"I hope we get there on time. You know how I hate to be late. With us leaving this close, maybe we should drive in my new 2014 Quartz, which gets you there in half the time?" Wendy replies.

"No, we shouldn't. You sound like one of those commercials. My turn of the century 1999 car will get us there just fine. Ole' Minnie here can handle anything. Besides, you know you're not used to the hydraulic speed on that thing yet. You need more practice getting around. I don't know why you let your father talk you into it anyway," Julie says driving down Cherry Street.

"Speaking of people talking me into something, how about this dress? I let you talk me into going to our 10th year high school reunion in a red dress! I should have my head examined! Maybe we should have worn my favorite color purple from our college days and childhood. You know red went out of style for women when we graduated 10 years ago. As a matter of fact, the only reason why you want us to wear red is because it's your favorite color. You want us to look alike, like we did in high school. In high school, we only wore red overalls or pants and matching shirts. Not red formal dresses! Although, I think my red dress is the prettiest," Wendy says with a smirk in her voice.

"You know red is one of our high school colors also. We won't be out of date with red on. I'll have to admit your red dress is prettier than mine's with those pearls on the top and the matching pearls on its jacket. Those gold shoes are 21st century and look great with that dress," Julie says.

"But it's only because you found the pattern for that dress first. I was going to copy you're old A-line style so that my dress would cover my hips very tightly in this sequence material. But I thought about my hips moving in a tight red dress. Yeah a tight red sequence dress might attract too much of the wrong type of attention, if you get what I mean. That is why I choose a different pattern even though I kept the red sequence material. I like this flare dress on my body. It hugs my breasts comfortably and fashionably. The dress is floor length like yours. Anyway, we wore your favorite color purple to the last five functions we attended together. So stop your gripping," says Julie.

"Yeah, you're right we did. We looked good then and we look good now," says Wendy.

Julie turns slowly onto the freeway, merges into traffic and then pushes her foot to the floor of her car as she accelerates to go over 120 miles to get to the Cheszer Hotel in Oakton, IL.

"We should be there in five minutes," says Julie while she's concentrating on the road. She swerves passed a 10-wheeler truck and swooshes by a man doing about 60 miles in the fast lane. Wendy braces herself by placing her hands on the dashboard in front of her.

"I think you need to slow down," says Wendy.

"And you wanted to drive your new 2014 Quartz!" says Julie.

Julie had her car altered to go at high speeds five years ago when the new Lee-May Converter hit the market. The Lee-May Converter was designed to update the 20th century cars so that they could go at high speeds like Wendy's new 2014 Quartz. People driving these new car types had to get used to the high speeds because many of them had been driving no faster than 55 to 65 miles an hour on a good day. Some people had even taken old-fashioned racecar lessons so that they could adjust to the new speeds. Wendy's father helped her purchase the new 2014 Quartz to keep her up to date. Wendy has not taken the high speed driving classes. She only drives at speeds of 55 to 60 miles per hour, which is very slow in today's fast moving world.

The music of the c.d. continues to play in the back ground and both women grow silent. Moving into the middle right lane where the speed limits were between 55 and 65 miles per hour, Julie slows her car down to 60 miles per hour.

Shifting her position, Wendy pulls down the mirror on the passenger side over the dashboard. She looks into the mirror at her makeup then reaches in her purse. Pulling out her eye shadow gel from her cosmetic bag, Wendy strokes her eyelids with eye shadow gel. Putting the eye shadow gel back into her cosmetic bag, she retrieves her oversized blush brush. Softly caressing her eyelids, Wendy blends the eye shadow over her eyelids. Glancing into the mirror a second time, she smiles at her reflection. Satisfied, Wendy replaces all the contents inside her cosmetic bag then puts the cosmetic bag back inside her purse. She removes her jacket and places both her purse and jacket on the back seat of the car. Closing her eyes for a moment, Wendy says,

"You know I think we're going to have a great time. I've been looking forward to this since I got my invitation. I just wish I could have worked on the reunion committee. I had so many things going on at work and church that I couldn't take on another commitment."

"I know what you mean. I wanted to write a poem or something to share with my old classmates. But I just didn't have the time either. I'm glad you got the invitation because they didn't even have my information. I guess I would not have known if it hadn't been for you being my roommate. Say, you think that they're even going to recognize you?" Julie asks giggling.

"I don't know? We'll have to see because my body hasn't changed," says Wendy as she giggles too.

"Oh, you know what I mean. Here we go again, giggling like we did when we were little children," says Julie with a chuckle.

Julie exists the freeway and turns onto the left ramp going south on Route 25. She can see the Cheszer Hotel up ahead. Slowing down to 35 miles, she reads silently the marquee. In large letters it says:

Welcome Preston High School Alumni Class of 2004

"We're here! Look, they even greet us in red lettering! I guess red is the color for tonight. We'll find out in a few moments whether or not our old classmates recognize me," says Wendy.

Julie drives close to a man standing near the front entrance of the Cheszer Hotel. She comes to a complete stop behind a midnight blue Dasher, with 30" magnum wheels and chrome rims. As the door of the Dasher opens, foldout portable steps spill out unto the walkway. A man, dressed in a red-hot, short-waist jacket over red-hot knee-length pants that have silver bells and streamers projecting from them, holds a hand out to the woman stepping out of the Dasher.

This must be the valet or bellmen service, Julie thinks. After helping the woman, the man walks around the back of the vehicle to the other side and opens the door on the driver's side. Exchanging the keys for a parking stub with the driver, a medium-height, black-haired man, the bellman jumps in the Dasher and drives it away. The man dressed in a cream-colored, linen texture zip-suit walks over and reaches for the arm of the woman whom had gotten out of the Dasher. She is dressed in a knee-length cream dress that is trimmed in gold, which sways softly as the wind gently blows against it. The woman not the man looks faintly familiar. The couple walks through the Cheszer Hotel doors and Julie wonders, are they going to the reunion also? If so, who are they?

Julie drives into the spot the Dasher was just at. A woman dressed in the same uniform reaches for the passenger door where Wendy sits. Hmm, Julie thinks "a valet or **bell person service**." The bell woman opens Wendy's door, helps Wendy out, then walks around the back of Julie's car to the driver's side and reaches for the car keys from Julie. As Julie takes off her house key from her key ring, she receives her parking stub and presents the car keys to the bell woman. Wendy gets her things out of the back seat.

"Just a minute," says Julie to the bell woman.

"I need to get some things out of the back seat before you park this car," says Julie.

"Okay, no problem," replies the bell woman. The bells on the bottom of her uniform jingle as she steps back to allow Julie room to reach in the back seat. Julie retrieves her purse, her camera, her short-waist red jacket and the film in a bag. Running her hand along her dress, Julie tugs quickly at the sides to remove creases that are trying to form in her dress. She does not want anything out of place when she sees her old classmates and their spouses or significant others.

Julie's mind wonders back to the woman, who got out of the Dasher in front of her and Wendy. The woman in the cream colored dress smiled when she glanced toward Julie and Wendy's direction. That smile changed to a brief worried look as the man with her hooked his arm into hers. Julie had seen this type of look before. Yet at the moment, she could not place her finger on whom or where? Julie had only gotten a glimpse of the woman's face. Yet, something else was nagging at Julie's conscious. The woman really looks familiar. Pausing, Julie stops walking to think. What is so familiar about that woman's look and her face? Perhaps she is an old classmate but she could not have changed that much, where she is unrecognizable, could she?

The fact that this woman is possibly an old classmate is not the issue, Julie thinks. It was the look on that woman's face, which is the problem. Then it hits Julie as to why the woman's look was so intriguing. She had seen a similar look on women, who were being battered by their husbands or boyfriends. The worried look reminded her of a distress signal, which says, "Help me!" Julie thinks.

As Julie reminisces further, her mind goes back to one such woman in college: Kim. Kim was madly in love with Chris. Chris was insanely jealous over Kim. Julie remembered talking with Kim about leaving Chris. At first, Kim could not find it in herself to leave Chris. Julie recalled how several times the police had to be called to stop Chris from hitting Kim. Each time Chris got of jail, he promised not to do it again. Kim fell for that same old line because Chris showed real tears and proclaimed how he could not live without Kim. Kim would not press charges against Chris. Things between Kim and Chris went fine for a while until some other man looked at Kim, especially when they socialized in groups where other men did not know that Kim and Chris were dating.

Chris always insisted that he and Kim go out and party. Many times, those parties turned into nightmares for Kim. Kim was so attractive that some man would walk up to Kim and ask her to dance. If Chris was out of the room or talking with other people a little distance away, she would just tell the man "No." If the man accepted that answer, then there was no problem. It became a problem if the man persisted and Chris returned to the room or came over from his other conversation and stood with Kim. At first, Chris asked Kim if she wanted to dance with the man. She immediately said, "No!" Then Chris might pick a fight with the other man for harnessing his woman. If Chris got into a fight with the other man, Kim stood on the side saying,

"Come on baby. It's nothing. You know I only want you. This man means nothing to me." Julie remembers.

Generally, her comments went along those lines. Once the fight was broken up, Chris danced with Kim for the rest of the night holding her very close. If Chris had not gotten over his anger during the party, he grabbed Kim's arm and roughly Chris escorted her home early from the party. After this pattern happened a few times, Kim got a particular look on her face. It was a fearful look, which said:

"I don't know what's going to happen next. **HELP ME!**"

Julie reminisces further. Once we were wise to the "look," different students attempted to calm Chris down because they knew the consequences if they did not. The first time people on Chris' dorm floor heard Kim screaming and crying from within Chris' dorm room, security and the police were called. After a while, security kept a pass key so they could immediately enter into Chris' room after receiving so many complaints from other residents of the dorm, whom heard Kim shouting things like,

"I didn't start talking with him!"

Or

"I don't know who that guy was! Please don't hit me! I didn't do nothing!"

After a while, residents of the dorm did not hear Kim screaming but instead they heard a lot of loud thumping and crashing noises. Once those noises settled down, Chris' room remained quiet for a long time. Then dorm residents sitting in the lobby or on the same floor would be shocked when Kim later emerged from Chris' room being escorted with assistance to her own dorm room. Kim's face would be swollen and covered with bluish-black marks. She wore a skullcap, which covered her hair and a couple of times her jacket was torn. Generally, Chris' attempts to get Kim back to her dorm room unnoticed after he checked to see that no one was around: failed. There were so many students that Chris could not control, who saw what. The other dorm residents complained again and again. Julie remembers.

The Resident Attendant (RA) on the floor got wise to Chris and called security any time there were any noises coming from Chris' room. As soon as security knocked on Chris' door, all the thumping noises stopped. Shuffling noises were heard right before Chris answered the door. Chris opened the door but stepped out of his room. Security asked to see Kim. Chris said she was in bed. Security insisted on waiting until Kim came to the door and said things were all right. If Chris did not answer the door quickly enough, then security used their pass key to enter Chris' room. If Kim's face was disfigured from physical blows she could not have inflicted on herself, security escorted Chris off campus to the local authorities. If Kim looked okay, security requested Kim leave. Next security escorted Kim to her dorm room.

A meeting on "how to handle Chris" was attended by all the RA's. Julie just happened to be a RA that year and was asked if she would talk to Kim to find out why she did not scream when Chris was beating her. This was something Julie wanted to know anyway. Julie asked Wendy to pray along with her on the best way to approach Kim. It was suggested that when Julie talked with Kim to try to get Kim to press charges against Chris, for her not to enter Chris' dorm room and see if Kim would go for some counseling. Julie remembers.

Julie had to find a way to build confidence between Kim and herself. Julie became the real female friend Kim had difficulty finding on campus, others only talked about her and Chris' issues behind Kim's back. After having a few prayer sessions with Wendy, Julie felt impressed by God to tell Kim about her own mother. That was hard because it was the second time Julie discussed her own personal situation with another peer other than Wendy, who was her real friend. Julie prayed for strength from God to help her find the right time and the right moment.

At first, Julie sat with both Chris and Kim during meal times in the cafeteria or cafe on campus. Establishing a relationship took a while, especially since Chris was suspicious of any friendships that Kim possessed. He always thought they were talking about him at first. Slowly,

Chris trusted Kim and Julie to be alone together. After a while, Chris did not mind when Kim and Julie went shopping together, especially since Chris did not like shopping. Julie remembers.

The second time Kim and Julie went shopping, Kim wore oversized dark glasses and a large scarf just like Julie's mama used to wear. Julie noticed that Kim was walking a little stiffly too. It was during this time that Julie treated Kim to lunch and told Kim how Julie's daddy used to beat her mama. Julie discussed the fear she used to have as a little girl when her daddy got angry. Julie explained that when her mama left her daddy, things changed for them both. Julie did not live in fear any more.

Julie explained that other than Wendy she only shared this information with the counselor at the shelter they moved to and the only other person in the world, who understood how she felt: Jesus. The counselor and her relationship with Jesus helped Julie realize that children did not have to live in fear like she had. Jesus and the counselor helped Julie to realize that **if a man hits a woman it is not love**. Kim had a few questions. Julie remembers them as if it was yesterday. One question was:

"How could Jesus and the counselor talk to you at the same time?" asked Kim.

"Well, I prayed and asked Jesus, why does my daddy hit my mama? I also asked Jesus: does my daddy really love my mama? Then I got quiet and listened real hard for an answer from Jesus. Later when I was reading my bible, I read the chapter on love, which is 1 Corinthians 13. Two of the verses provided my answers and really helped me. The fourth verse in the King James Bible says:

"Charity suffereth long and is kind; charity envieth

not; charity vaunteth not itself, is not puffed up"
(1 Corinthians 13:4 KJV), 'And the fifth verse says:'
"Doth not behave itself unseemly, seeketh not her
own, is not easily provoked, thinketh no evil"
(1 Corinthians 13:5 KJV);

"First of all each time it says charity, it means love. I had heard this many times in church services. Secondly as I thought about these two scriptures, the one thing that stood out in my mind was the part which says, now I'm substituting 'love' for 'charity' so bear with me as I say this. But the part that stood out in my mind was love suffereth long and is kind. I thought about all those times my daddy was not kind to my mama. (Julie remembers.)

"The next part which got me was '... *is not easily provoked, thinketh no evil' (1 Corinthians 13:5b KJV).* I remember my daddy coming home one time and I told him how this man asked my mama directions to our school. She gave the man pretty good directions. My daddy got so mad that he hit my mama for flirting with another man. I was so sorry. I didn't get a chance to tell my daddy that the man Mama gave directions to; was with his wife and children. I didn't discuss anything after that with Daddy unless I talked with Mama first," Julie said.

"So when the counselor talked to me about how real love does not beat someone, I heard parts of that scripture in my head from Jesus at the same time. Hearing it like that validated what the counselor was saying," I said. (Julie remembers.)

"Oh, I see," Kim replied.

"Just to make sure I was thinking right and since the Bible I was looking in had all those 'eth's, I decided to look up the scriptures in a different translation. I looked up those same verses in the New International Bible. It read,

"Love is patient, love is kind. It does not envy, it does not boast, it is not proud. It does not dishonor others, it is not self-seeking, it is not easily angered, it keeps no record of wrongs"
(1 Corinthians 13:4-5 NIV), Julie said.

I remember telling Kim I wanted to make sure I had everything clear. So I looked up the same scriptures one more time in the New Living Translation Bible (NLT). That version said:

"Love is patient and kind. Love is not jealous or boastful or proud or rude. It does not demand its own way. It is not irritable, and it keeps no record of being wronged" (1 Corinthians 13:4-5 NLT).

I told Kim I realized that Jesus was talking to me through me hearing those scripture selections at the same time the counselor was talking to me. Jesus and the counselor were saying the same things.

I also explained to Kim how the counselor and Jesus helped me see that God had provided an example for me of a family where the children did not live in fear: my friend, Wendy's family. I said it was during this time that I realized God had provided a real true friend that I could talk to besides Jesus: Wendy. Julie remembers.

Julie told Kim how she finally told Wendy her secret about her mama and her daddy right before Julie and her mama moved. Julie also explained how Wendy did not tell anyone until Julie told her it was okay. And how once Mama and Daddy were divorced, Mama had her name changed from Julie Perez to Rosita Lee. It took a while to adjust but now I have two cool names: Julie for grammar school and college and Rosita for high school and part of college.

Julie explained that she and Wendy connected again after Wendy's family moved to Chicago. Wendy went to the same high school she did. Julie remembers.

It was at this point that Kim realized she could confide in Julie as a true friend. So Kim shared one of her secrets. Kim admitted that her daddy beat her mama too. Kim admitted she used to be terrified as a child also. But she loved her daddy. Kim's daddy and mother are still together right now today. Her daddy was not the only one, who hits his wife; her brothers hit their wives. And her sister's husband hits her. Kim admitted that she figured it was just normal.

Kim relaxed enough to tell Julie how Chris hit her and she didn't make a sound. When he was real angry, Chris grabbed her and taped her mouth up so that she did not scream when he was hitting her. Because he started differently each time, it caught her off guard most of the time. Kim admitted that she learned how unpredictable her relationship was with Chris. One moment he could be hugging and kissing her and in the next moment, he would be taping her mouth up and hitting her. Kim did not like the situation but she loved Chris. When he was not hitting her, Chris was kind and sweet, just like those scriptures said. Julie remembers.

Julie prayed and explained that no matter how sweet Chris was, **it was wrong for him to hit her**! Julie also told Kim that I know Mama is happier without Daddy. Julie suggested to Kim that she needed to make a decision. Julie encouraged Kim not go to Chris' dorm room with him. If she felt like Chris was going to hit her, Kim was to give Julie some type of signal. Kim explained that if she said anything to Chris or about Chris in front of other people than her butt whipping would be worse. Then Kim decided that if Julie was around, Kim could give Julie a smile with a worried look. The look would send out a distress signal, which said,

"I don't know what's going to happen next. **Help me**!"

Julie agreed to do whatever she could to help Kim at that moment without endangering herself. Julie remembers.

That afternoon took a long time. So much time that Julie looked up and she saw Chris walking through the mall a few stores away from the restaurant. Chris was looking in windows searching for them. Julie changed the subject and started talking about her new shoes she had just purchased. Kim commented on Julie's shoes and the great sale price Julie paid for her shoes. Kim was completely engrossed in suggesting which outfits Julie's shoes would match when Chris walked into the restaurant and over to their table. Julie thanked Jesus for letting her see Chris before he saw them. Julie made a mental note to get a booth further back in the restaurant the next time they talked.

Julie kept her promise with Kim. From that point on, Julie and her friends were able to avert Chris from hitting Kim. Whenever Julie saw a smile and that worried look on Kim's face, Julie went into action of getting her friends to distract Chris long enough to get Kim out of there. Initially a few of the guys, who were Julie's friends, talked Chris into going somewhere without Kim. This worked because Chris would not hit them and Chris depended on Julie to make sure Kim got home. Julie remembers.

In the meantime, Julie and Wendy prayed a lot about Kim's situation. They prayed that Chris realized it was wrong to hit Kim and for Kim to realize it was wrong for her to be hit. Julie even called a few prayer groups and asked them to pray for a woman on her college campus. Julie talked with Kim whenever possible.

One night Chris did not respond to the guys trying to distract him. Kim gave Julie the look and when Julie asked Chris if she could drive Kim home, Chris refused. He angrily grabbed Kim's arm and pulled her out of the party. People followed Chris and watched as he attempted to shove Kim into his car so that she would go with him back to his dorm room. When Kim resisted and broke free of Chris, he chased her down the street in front of everyone. She had no shoes on. That night Chris over powered Kim and it took a few guys to pull Chris off of Kim. Someone had already called campus security and the local police. Julie remembers.

It took a lot of prayer and talking to get Kim to leave Chris and press charges against Chris. Kim finally realized that what Chris had been doing to her, what had been happening at home with her parents, with her sister and with her sister-in-laws: **was wrong**! Kim finally made a decision that night, which saved her life.

Kim eventually changed colleges and Chris got a new girlfriend, who was younger than Kim. The new girlfriend was not as blessed as Kim. The new girlfriend hit her head on the dresser as she fell one night while Chris was hitting her after he taped shut her mouth. She died when her neck snapped. Chris is in jail now for that. The new girlfriend had developed the same look but she trusted no one and confided in no one. None of us could get close enough to her to help her. Julie remembers.

The look, the fearful look that Kim used to have was

similar to the look that this woman in the cream dress had for a brief moment when that man grasped her arm. I hope I see this woman again so that I may find out if my suspicions are accurate. I don't want to see another woman go through the same things Kim went through nor Chris' last girlfriend. Julie thinks.

Julie's hesitation in deep thought and standing still is a bit too long. So long that Wendy stops walking, turns around and says,

"Julie, I thought we're here to go to a reunion. I didn't get dressed up to go by myself nor watch you daydream in the middle of a walkway. Come on. I spent a lot of money on this dress and I want to get to the reunion!"

Snapping out of her college days, Julie focuses on Wendy.

"Oh, I'm coming. Wait for me," says Julie. Still thinking about the woman, Julie prays.

"Father God, if you want me to talk with this woman please provide an opportunity for me to see her. I hope she is at our reunion so I don't have to search all over the hotel for her. I would not know where to begin. If she is not at this reunion, then Father God, would you let me run into her please? I know you hear my prayers, so could you give me what to say to her when I encounter her. Please give me the right words, the right tone and help me to do it in love, in Jesus' name amen."

Julie knows her prayer is heard. She quickens her steps to catch up with Wendy. Julie thinks for a moment, maybe Wendy can help with this. I'll have to see. I just need to find that woman, who needs my help, Julie thinks.

Chapter 8
The Woman

Julie catches up with Wendy. Glancing around for signs to follow to the ballroom, the two women walk through the atrium of the Cheszer Hotel. Adjusting their eyes to being inside, they stop for a moment to drink in the sight. In the center of the atrium is a pond. As they stroll a little closer to the pond, they see some huge rare white catfish swimming around inside. Large palm trees encircle the pond. Old-fashioned white wire tables each with a set of four matching chairs surround the pond. The table sets remind Julie of the quaint one her maternal grandmother had when she was younger. These antiques must have cost the Cheszer Hotel a pretty penny because the metal used to produce them is scarce these days as are a lot of raw materials.

Over to the right of the pond is an entrance with a sign, which beckons people to stroll down the cinnamon colored brick pavement. Attached to this entrance are 12' tall white velour drapes, which look like two huge "R's" opposite each other. Golden ropes encircle the bend in the "R's" and are tautly drawn creating puffiness in the middle part of the "R." Golden tassels line the hem of the drapes. An overhead sign indicates this is the actual hotel lobby entrance.

Right behind the pond, is another doorway. This doorway has crimson steel doors with large hexagon gold knobs. A wide roll of gold velour is meticulously placed over the entryway with a circular gold knob at each end. Long thin gold colored velour drapes hang on each side of the door. This 1970 window treatment effect draws attention to the golden-reddish pavement leading to this entry. The sign leading to this entrance says: "The Fire Inn." This is the hotel's bar. At this point Julie notices that not only is the pond the center of this atrium but the pavement surrounding and leading up to the pond encompasses a mixture of colors.

The pavement encircling the pond itself has cinnamon and gold colored bricks and white stones. The white stones cut like bricks shine as if they are polished daily. The white stones exit left from the pond out of the atrium and lead to the Cheszer Hotel's Royal Ballroom door. Strategically disbursed throughout the atrium are comfortable oversized gold colored chairs covered with the same soft velour fabric as the drapes. An enormous banner with red lettering and gray shadows hangs from the ceiling near the ballroom entrance saying:

Wendy and Julie walk in this direction. Breaking the silence, Wendy says,

"Julie, did you see that woman with that man? Didn't she look familiar to you?"

"Yeah, her face is familiar. She reminds me of someone but I can't quite put my finger on who? Maybe, she's one of our classmates. That guy with her is a hunk! But I don't think anyone could have changed that much where they would be unrecognizable. What do you think?" Julie asks Wendy.

"Yeah, he is kind of cute. I don't know. You remember

when I saw Jerry a few weeks ago?" Wendy asks.

"Jerry, who?" asks Julie.

"You know the boy, who ran after Peter almost every day at the bus stop when we were in seventh grade. He was my old boyfriend after you left," Wendy says.

"Oh yeah: him. Yeah, that's right. When you visited your grandmother where we used to live, you saw him and he asked you, if you were Wendy's cousin? Once he realized it was you, he asked you out on a date," Julie responds with a chuckle in her voice.

Flipping her hair, as they rapidly step towards the reception table outside of the ballroom hall, Wendy asks,

"What is so funny about him wanting to take me out? He has grown into a good looking hunk. Besides…"

Distracted Wendy stops talking as a tall thin, 6'3" guy walks up to Julie. He had just finished getting his nametag from the registration table behind the red and white banner. He places his hand over his nametag. While he looks a little familiar, Wendy's mouth drops as he speaks to Julie.

"Rosita… Rosita Lee, is that you?" he asks.

Julie turns and looks the guy directly in the face. She cannot place him but his face looks very familiar. Wendy says out loud,

"Percy! Percy is that you?"

Julie jumps back and says,

"You are not Percy! You can't be Percy. The last time I saw Percy, he was shorter than me," Rosita/Julie says.

"Yes it is me: Percy Lee Jackson in the flesh! I grew taller in undergrad. You guys look great though. Still wearing red I see," Percy says as he removes his hand from covering his nametag.

"If she's Rosita, then you must be Wendy! I like the

hair color! Actually, I'm kidding. I recognized you right away, Ms. Wendy!" says Percy.

Rosita is at a loss for words. Percy her old lab partner from chemistry and biology is standing taller than both her and Wendy! Besides that: he looks good! Wow! Tall and slim in a nice blue professional suit over his spit polished, matching blue leather shoes with a light blue buttoned collared shirt wearing a great looking blue patterned tie. Rosita thinks as she looks him up and down.

"You sure you're not an imposter. The Percy I knew was my lab partner in biology. Maybe you're his cousin and came to the reunion in his place. Percy always talked about his cousin and his favorite color being blue or red. Is Percy sick or something?" asks Rosita/Julie.

"I remember that Julie. You're right! He's wearing a blue suit, a nice blue suit! I think it is Percy himself. Besides look at his face closely, it still has that baby face he had when he was in high school. It's just not as round," Wendy says chuckling.

Julie looks at Percy's face. Nodding she says:

"It is Percy Lee Jackson!"

"Wendy, why did you call her Julie? I thought her name is Rosita," states Percy. Wendy looks at Julie and Julie looks back at Wendy and smiles. Finally Julie's high school secret is revealed Wendy thinks. Julie/Rosita smiles and says,

"I'll answer that question."

"Yes she called me Julie. It's my name. It's a long story but here is the short version. My name is both Julie and Rosita. Mama and I left a bad family situation before I attended Preston High School. We changed my birth name legally from Julie to Rosita to protect my mom and me.

Wendy and I used to be best friends in grammar school and junior high where we used to live.

"She knew my history and my past. That day she entered our biology class was the first time I had seen her in three years. I hoped she did not shout out "Julie" in front of everyone. As my best friend reconnected, Wendy kept the secret of my birth name all throughout high school," says Rosita/Julie.

Percy looks at Rosita then at Wendy. Quiet for a moment as if he is lost in time, Percy excitedly says,

"So that's why you two became such close friends so quickly! I remember the day after you, Wendy came to our school that both of you wore purple outfits the very next day. It puzzled me for the longest time.

"I couldn't understand how you bonded so quickly? And the day after that you both wore red to school, which is Rosita's favorite color like you knew each other from the beginning of freshman year. Then the two of you were always in a corner or off alone somewhere whispering and laughing like you were telling each other secrets nobody else knew. Whenever anyone walked too close to you, the two of you stopped talking about things and just stared at the person like they interrupted something sacred.

"Wow, so this was your high school secret that Wendy kept for you: that your birth name is Julie," says Percy.

"Wow that's some secret you have Rosita. So what do you want me to call you: Julie or Rosita?" asks Percy.

"Rosita is fine. No one else at Preston High will know who I am if you call me something different. Besides, I have gotten used to being called either name. It's okay that you know me as Julie and call me Rosita," Julie says.

Looking directly at Wendy, Percy asks,

"Did you ever tell her my secret I shared with you that day in honors chemistry when Rosita was absent from class? Or were you my real friend too? I needed a friend that day."

Wendy blinks her eyes then shuts them completely to remember what in the world Percy is talking about? Rosita stands there looking puzzled because she can't remember any secret that Wendy told her about Percy.

The only secret Rosita knew about Percy was he liked Wendy from the day he met her. Percy told her one day in the hallway on their way to English class that Wendy was going to be his wife. With all the things Percy did in high school, Rosita didn't think that would ever happen especially with Percy being so much shorter than Wendy. So she just prayed God's will for Wendy and Percy. Who knows if Percy was supposed to be Wendy's husband? They were both her friends throughout high school. Only God knew what was in His plans for Wendy and Percy. That is why Rosita prayed.

Rosita never told Wendy Percy's secret because he asked her not to tell Wendy. As a friend, Rosita knew how important it was to keep a secret for a friend. Wendy put her hand over her mouth and slowly nodded her head. Wendy says,

"Oh, my I almost forgot that day. No I never told Rosita. But I did tell Jesus. From that day forward I prayed for you and your family every day until we graduated. I knew that God answered my prayers again when I saw your dad at our graduation and him hugging you.

"You looked surprised yourself that he was there. I even saw your two sisters and your mom take pictures with you and your dad afterwards. I'm glad it all turned out well for you and your family," says Wendy.

"Wow, you must be a very, very close friend to God. My mom went from kicking my dad out of the house in our junior year of high school to letting him come back home when I started my freshman year of college. She called a lawyer and everything my junior year. Initially, my sisters were going to have to decide, which parent they wanted to live with after I graduated from high school. Mom was selling the house, moving out of state to wherever her job would transfer her to and divorcing my dad. Over done! That was the end of story at first. Mom wouldn't even let Dad talk, apologize or nothing," says Percy.

"Your prayers worked because Mom went to this church about a month later and received Jesus in her heart. By the end of our junior year, Mom and Dad went to marriage counseling. Remember all those times I left school a little early in our senior year?" asks Percy. Wendy and Rosita both nod their heads.

"Well those were the days we all went to family counseling. Dad and I began talking more. Our relationship changed. He played basketball with me after school and even took me to a few major league basketball games at night. I was surprised Dad made it to my graduation because at first he couldn't get the time off work at his new job. And at the last minute they released him," says Percy.

Turning to Rosita, he winks at her and asks,

"Did you ever tell Wendy my secret I shared with you?"

Wendy interrupts.

"Wait... Wait... Wait a minute before you answer Rosita. So you had a secret with both Rosita and me?" asks Wendy. Percy and Rosita laugh. Then he says,

"Yes I did. My secret with Rosita was a little different though. It wasn't about my family. I remember somebody telling someone else's family business from freshman year. Although my family secret was not as bad as their secret, the whole freshman class knew about it and talked about it.

"Thank you for not sharing my family business in high school. I never heard a word from anyone. I thought you might tell Rosita since the two of you whispered so much! The secret I told Rosita was about you," says Percy.

Rosita nods her head, looks at Wendy and smiles. Placing her hand on her chest with a startled expression on her face, Wendy pulls her head back a little. She asks,

"About me???"

"Yes, it was about you: Ms. Wendy. Look I'll let you guys get registered, get your nametags and pick up your gifts. I'll go secure a table for us to sit at because I desire to continue this conversation. If that's okay with you two," says Percy.

Wendy looks at the two of them smiling like that Cheshire cat with the big grin on his face in the fairy tales. Taking a deep breath she says,

"It's okay. I didn't even know there was a secret about me all these years. I guess I can wait a few more minutes to hear this secret."

Percy heads into the ballroom while Wendy and Rosita go register. They register and pick up their gifts. Walking towards the ballroom door, Rosita sees the woman in the cream dress, who got out that car with that look on her face go to the back of the line to register for the reunion. She is standing right next to that man holding her arm very tightly.

Giving Wendy her gift, purse and her jacket to take to the table; Rosita excuses herself from Wendy. Rosita tells Wendy she will find her inside. Wendy takes the stuff and goes looking for Percy. She wants to know: what the other secret is both of them were smiling about?

Rosita waits for the registration line to go down. She takes a few pictures. She makes small talk with the reunion committee and people as they register. She desires to know, who is this woman and if she can help her?

As the woman gets closer to Rosita, she keeps trying to place her face. It hits her right as the woman signs in. No it couldn't be who she thinks it is? Why that means this woman would have lost over 100 pounds since high school. Looking at this woman's face one last time, Rosita says out loud,

"Florence, Florence French! Is that you?"

The woman's face brightens. She hugs Rosita and smiles.

"Yes it's me, Rosita Lee. How are you? I didn't think anybody would recognize me. But you were always good with people and their faces. I recognized you right away. By the way this is my fiancé: Walter," says Florence.

"Walter: this is my classmate Rosita. We were friends in high school. We had some classes together," Florence says introducing the man clinging tightly to her arm. Walter extends his free hand to Rosita. He mumbles,

"Pleased to meet you." Rosita extends her hand, and says,

"Pleased to meet you." She shakes his hand and quickly snatches her hand back.

Walter is a dirty dog. He just thrust his middle finger in my palm while shaking my hand, Rosita thinks. She frowns while he gives her a weird smile. The last time a man did that to me I asked God about it. God said "the man is making a pass at you." The problem was that first man was married to a friend of mine. Now this man did it and he's Florence's fiancé? Florence's fiancé just made a pass at me! I'm glad Florence didn't see his face, Rosita thinks.

"Is Wendy here too? Do you think she'll recognize me?" asks Florence.

"Yes, she's here. I was just going to find her. We came together. We went to college together. You may not recognize her. I don't know if she'll recognize you. I knew you longer than she did. We both have on red dresses. Her dress is prettier than mine though. Who knows? Maybe Wendy will recognize you right away," says Rosita.

Rosita heads for the door to the ballroom. Florence and Walter are close behind her at first. Catching up, Florence continues talking.

"I would like to see Wendy again. Wendy was always nice to me in school. As a matter of fact, Wendy prayed for me to lose all the weight I lost, one day in our honors Spanish class right before we graduated. She also prayed I would find a man to get married to and here I am engaged to Walter. Let me know where you guys are sitting so I can talk with Wendy. Okay?" says Florence.

"Girl you know I will. I'm sure Wendy wants to see you as well. I don't know where they are?" says Rosita.

"They? Who are they?" asks Florence.

"Oh I forgot to tell you. We ran into Percy when we got here. He and Wendy are waiting for me at a table wherever it is," says Rosita.

"Oh they are. Okay well, I'll see you in a few minutes

once Walter and I get settled," Florence says. Rosita goes ahead searching for the table where Wendy and Percy are. Walter and Florence stand still inside the door of the ballroom.

"Well Walter do you want to sit with them or is there some place else you see for us to sit?" asks Florence.

Walter's eyes squint while looking around the room. Tables fill up quickly as the people come in. Close to the dance floor is a couple at a table waving their arms beckoning towards their direction. That must be them Walter thinks until they stop waving when the couple standing next to Walter and Florence wave back to them. I guess it's not them, he thinks.

Walter watches the path Rosita walks. She stops and sits at a table also near the dance floor where two people are already seated but not waving their arms. That Rosita is fine! Walter relaxes his hold on Florence's arm for a moment. I guess it wouldn't hurt to be the only other guy at that table. Walter thinks.

"We can sit with your friends. I see them other there close to the dance floor. Maybe we can get some dancing in," says Walter.

Rosita makes it to the table before anyone else does. Percy and Wendy don't even look up when Rosita sits down next to Wendy. This is strange, Rosita thinks. The two of them possess these creamy looks facing each other. They didn't even hear me walk up nor do they hear me now! Then Rosita realizes and hears from God. Oh my God! He's the one! Rosita thinks.

"Guys, guys. Earth to you two, I'm here. I've got news for you two," says Rosita.

"We've got news for you too. Wendy just agreed to

marry me," says Percy. Tears roll down Wendy's face.

Rosita jumps up, grabs Wendy and hugs her. Then the two women scream and jump together with tears streaming down both their faces. Rosita releases Wendy. She reaches over grabs Percy, pulls him out of his chair and hugs him. She releases him and goes back to hugging Wendy again. Percy slumps into his chair.

After the two women scream one last time, Rosita goes and sits in her chair next to Wendy. Other classmates have burst out in screams and shouts as they recognized one another so people think the people at Rosita and Wendy's table are doing the same.

Dark mascara paints their faces. Wendy's right eye has heavy black-brown marks under it liked someone hit her in it. Rosita's black mascara runs from both her eyes to her chin. It is ugly! Just as they quiet down, Florence and Walter walk over. Sitting down at the partially empty table, they look at the two women and laugh. Rosita looks at Wendy's face and Wendy looks at Rosita's face and they laugh as well. The whole table laughs loudly. Florence introduces Walter, her fiancé to Percy and Wendy.

Excusing themselves to the restroom to correct their makeup, they ask Florence if she wants to come along? All the ladies exit the table leaving the men to fend for themselves. After they leave, Brandon (the high school basketball hero) sits down with his date leaving three seats open at the table. Brandon and his date wear color matching outfits.

Percy introduces Walter, Florence's fiancé to Brandon. Brandon introduces his wife, Roberta to both men. Percy and Brandon catch up on old news from high school and what they are doing today. Roberta happy to see her husband talking with an old classmate removes Brandon's camera from her purse and takes pictures of the two men. Percy then takes pictures of Brandon and Roberta with Brandon's camera.

Walter smiles and looks impatiently at his watch. Walter says,

"Those women are taking a long time in the restroom."

"Huh! You think this is a long time?" asks Brandon. "You should have been with us at Preston High. Whenever Wendy and Rosita got together it was a deep and long conversation. Now they have Florence with them. They'll come back but they may stop and talk with several other women along the way," says Brandon.

"You're right about that!" says Percy.

"You remember the time we had that fire drill and everyone had to leave the building? Wendy and Rosita were so engrossed in their conversation that they did not hear the English teacher, Ms. Davis, who told us it was okay to go back into the building. The two of them were still talking and ignoring everyone else. Ms. Davis walked over to those two sitting on the ground on the other side of that huge tree across the street. Ms. Davis stood over them until they looked up and realized that everyone else was reentering the building. We laughed and teased them about that for a long time," says Percy.

"I remember that! So they are probably in the restroom talking about old times and they have Florence with them, who is engaged to you: Walter. Man let's just hope they return and leave those deep conversations behind.

"Or maybe you should have been at my house when Roberta was getting ready for tonight and her sister called. The two of them talked about what Roberta was wearing, which purse she was taking and what shoes matched! No matter that we are wearing color matching outfits that Roberta made especially for tonight. She didn't ask me what wallet I was taking or which shoes matched my outfit," says Brandon. The guys all laugh and Roberta smiles.

"I rushed my sister-in-law off the phone so that my beautiful wife could finish dressing and we could make it here. I promised my sister-in-law pictures of us, which is the only way I got her off the phone," says Brandon as he kisses his wife on the cheek.

"You got to know that women take time to look beautiful, a long long time. And sometimes they talk the whole time they are beautifying themselves," says Percy.

"As the only woman left at the table, I think we can safely say they will be back. I think y'all should change the subject as I'm not going to continue listening to you guys bashing women," says Roberta.

"All right sweetheart," says Brandon.

Turning to the guys at the table, Brandon says,

"You know how it is guys. I've got to please the woman in my life and I don't mind it at all. Let's change the subject to better things like: did you see Chicago's football team last season? I thought they would finally make it to the championship or at least come in third place."

"Yeah Man, third place would have been... (he pauses) nice," says Walter. Turning his head, he watches a woman walking by their table. Percy and Brandon look at each other. Roberta doesn't notice it as she is checking out a different woman at an adjacent table on the left side of them. Walter hears the lull in the conversation and responds.

"My bad... uh, what did you say?" asks Walter.

"Nothing Man we were only talking about the best team

in Chicago that needs to live up to their reputation," says Percy.

"Excuse me for a minute. I think that's Arlene from college over at that other table. I'll be right back," says Roberta. She leaves the table and goes to speak to the woman at the adjacent table. The two of them shout together and talk for a few minutes. Roberta brings Arlene back to the table to meet Brandon.

Arlene is married to John, their classmate. John went outside to get their camera from their car. Arlene is a healthy plus-sized woman wearing a rose tea length dress. Arlene is sure that John will be glad to see them and take pictures of them as soon as he gets back. Roberta insists that she and Arlene take pictures. Brandon uses his camera and takes pictures of Roberta and Arlene. Afterward Arlene smiles at everyone and goes back to her table. When John returns, he and Arlene come to the table to take more pictures.

Chapter 9
The Intervention

Rosita, Florence and Wendy excitedly walk to the restroom chatting with Florence about her weight loss. Wendy and Rosita congratulate Florence and thank God for her victory.

Entering the restroom, at first the women are alone. Then other women filter in and the place fills up as women use the facilities before dinner is served. The three of them decide to use the facilities and talk while correcting their makeup. After relieving themselves and washing their hands, Rosita and Wendy remove the smudged and running mascara. Florence freshens up her makeup and Wendy asks Florence questions about her life. While those two talk, Rosita remains silent.

So many thoughts race through Rosita's head. Although I am excited for Wendy, I know God answered my prayer to talk with the woman in the cream dress. Here she is right before me. I'm not sure where or how to start.

I believe I'll ask Wendy questions about her engagement when we get back at our apartment. There is so much to talk about as God is manifesting Himself in all areas tonight. My focus for now should be how to talk with Florence alone before the night is over. And with so many people around how am I going to do that? Rosita thinks.

"God I need your help right now," says Rosita out loud.

Wendy stops talking with Florence. She turns to Rosita and asks,

"Is everything okay, Rosita?"

"Yes it is," says Rosita.

"I was just whispering a prayer and did not intent for it

to be loud enough for everyone to hear," says Rosita.

"Oh, okay," says Wendy and returns to her conversation with Florence. It takes a different turn as Wendy asks Florence, how long has she known Walter? Where did Florence meet him? How did Walter propose to Florence? There are other questions that Rosita just listens to as Florence answers them. It is as if God is using Wendy to give Rosita information for her conversation alone with Florence later this evening. This is amazing, thinks Rosita.

Back at the table Roberta decides to go to the restroom leaving the men to fend at the table for themselves. She invites Arlene to go with her and they both head in a different direction than the other women went. The men talk while the women are gone. At first it is about sports, then the conversation changes after Brandon reveals he hurt his knee in college. He found out he has a rare medical condition which prevents Brandon from playing his heart: basketball. Percy then takes charge of the conversation questioning Walter about his relationship with Florence.

This is my opportunity to find out as much about Walter as possible, thinks Percy. I felt a little uncomfortable when Walter shook my hand. It is as if God is giving me a warning that something is not right about Walter. When I told God this is none of my business, God reminded me what a good friend Florence was to me in high school. Then the scripture came to me about real friends. The one that says:

"Faithful are the wounds of a friend; but the kisses
of an enemy are deceitful" (Proverbs 27:6 KJV).
It keeps playing over and over in my head. "Okay God I agree to do whatever it is you would have for me to do," whispers Percy.

Now that I have submitted to God, the scripture stopped playing over and over in my mind. I have been observing this Walter since he sat down. This is really peculiar. Walter's head turns every time a woman walks by the table. And he did this when Florence was sitting at the table before she went to the restroom with Wendy and Rosita. Percy thinks.

It's like Walter can't even focus on the conversation when any shapely woman or a woman in a tight dress walks by this table. It's so obvious since he watches where the woman goes, turns his head and follows her behind with his eyes until she sits down. And this is the man engaged to a nice woman like Florence? Something is wrong with this picture, thinks Percy.

Brandon notices that Walter cannot focus on the conversation when a woman walks by in a tight fitting dress. I'm getting tired of reeling this Walter back into the conversation. He has the attention span of a toddler, thinks Brandon.

Walter takes control of the conversation revealing his thoughts. "Man did you see that? I wonder what she's like in bed?" says Walter.

"Walter are you sure you're ready to get married to Florence?" asks Brandon.

"Huh? What do you mean?" asks Walter.

"Well, you keep looking at these women's behinds and you say you are engaged to Florence? When I got engaged to Roberta, I only had eyes for her. I did not care how many tight fitting behinds walked right by my face. The only behind I was interested in **and** am still interested in today is Roberta's! She's my woman! I approved her tight fitting dress 'cause she works hard to keep her shape and desires to show it off. I like walking into a place like this with my good looking woman on my arm. I don't want to see you looking at Roberta's behind or watching her behind while I'm dancing with her. **It's guys like you that make a married man want to fight**," says Brandon.

"Woe... woe Man I don't mean no harm. Just because I'm engaged don't mean I don't have eyes. I'm just looking," says Walter.

"We all have eyes. We just see where your eyes have been going since you sat down," says Percy.

"I agree with Brandon. You may want to reevaluate your decision about getting married to Florence. You may not be ready just yet," says Percy.

Walter sits there with a strange look on his face staring at Percy and Brandon. The men are so engrossed in their conversation that they do not notice the women returning to the table. After leaving Arlene with her husband at the adjacent table, Roberta comes back at that moment. Roberta sits down the same time as Rosita, Wendy, and Florence slide into their chairs.

"May not be ready just yet for what?" asks Roberta.

"Oh just men talk Baby," says Brandon. Then he kisses her on her cheek. Brandon introduces Roberta as his wife to Rosita, Wendy and Florence. Turning to Roberta and looking her directly in her eyes, Brandon asks,

"Do you want a drink?"

"May I go with you to select the one I desire, Sweetie?" asks Roberta.

"Anything for you Sweetheart, excuse us," says Brandon.

Pulling her chair back and offering his arm to her as she stands, Brandon and Roberta leave the table to head for the open bar. Brandon looks back to see if he has to deal with Walter staring at his wife's behind. Walter is wrapping his arms around Florence and staring into her eyes. Good, Brandon thinks. I would hate to have to whup a man right here in the middle of this **nice high school reunion** over my wife.

While Brandon and Roberta are away, the reunion committee secures Quincy to say the grace over the food. The servers serve the food and everyone starts eating. Between bites of food, Florence tells them of her colors for her wedding and that it is set for next year. Florence shares with them that Walter desires to get married sooner but that is the only date available at the location they selected. Brandon and Roberta return with their soda drinks since there was a variety of sodas on the bar and they do not drink any alcohol.

Camellita and her date come while the soup is being served. When they sit down, it leaves only one chair left for someone to occupy at their table. Camellita introduces her fiancé, Jeremiah to everyone. Camellita used to be on the cheerleading squad and part of the chess club in high school. Camellita and Rosita used to be great friends in high school as Camellita's favorite color is red also. She is wearing an A-line knee length, bright red silk dress with an imitation diamond broach on each shoulder.

Jeremiah is wearing a black suit with a white shirt and a bold red tie. His tie and handkerchief are both bright red made of the same silk fabric as Camellita's dress.

Everyone continues eating after complimenting each other on their choice of colors and their selection of clothes. A third of the people wore red that night as it is one of their high school colors. During the meal, the reunion committee shows old high school pictures taken from freshman year through to graduation. Prizes are given out to the one, who has traveled the longest distance to attend; the one with the largest family; the one with the highest degree at that time, which is a doctorate; and the one, who has changed the most since high school, which is Florence French.

After the meal is finished, they open up the middle of the floor for dancing so that they can work off the food they have just eaten. Besides, it is rumored that they're having an old fashioned dance contest similar to the ones they had in high school. People limber up so they can do their special dance moves.

Brandon and Roberta hit the dance floor. Camellita and Jeremiah follow. After the first song, Brandon and Jeremiah switch dance partners. Walter finally gets his wish. He and Florence go to the dance floor so she can keep her beautiful figure. Walter will only let Florence dance with himself. Different men try to cut in and exchange their woman for Florence. Walter is not having it.

With all of them gone from the table, Rosita, Percy, and Wendy compare notes about Walter.

"Something is not right about that man. I am getting a strange feeling from God about him," says Wendy.

"So I'm not the only one, who thinks something is wrong. I... I... I'm not comfortable being alone with Walter. Florence seems very happy. I never saw Florence this happy in high school. I wish I had known her in college or at least we had kept contact. I don't know. Maybe I shouldn't say anything," says Rosita.

"Okay Rosita, what's wrong with Walter?" asks Wendy.

Rosita looks around to see if anyone is close enough to hear them talking. Rosita lowers her voice.

"Well, I didn't want to say anything but he made a pass at me when we shook hands," whispers Rosita.

"**He did what???**" says Wendy loudly.

"Lower you voice, Wendy," says Rosita.

"I don't want to hurt Florence. She went through a lot in high school with all the teasing about her weight. I'm glad she's happy. I believe I'm supposed to say something to her. But exactly what that is, is what I'm praying about," says Rosita.

"Rosita has a point about keeping things quiet. After I shook Walter's hand, God dealt with me about saying something to help a friend: Florence. She was a good friend to me in high school. God let me know that something was wrong with Walter. And you just confirmed it Rosita," says Percy.

"I don't know how much Florence has changed since high school but I do know I should warn her about Walter. We men noticed something when all the women left the table. To make it short before anyone returns to the table and before the song ends, Walter is not ready for marriage now," states Percy.

"Let's pray together right now before they come back here," says Percy.

The three grab each other's hands, lower their heads, close their eyes, and pray to God for guidance on what they are to do and what they are to say. They also ask God to prepare Florence's heart to hear what they say and send someone as a witness of the kind of person Walter really is. They open their eyes just as the song ends and the couples start walking toward their table. "God is good. We finished just in time," thinks Percy.

Across the room Twinkie, who was in the restroom when the prizes were announced, is scoping the ballroom with her eyes. Twinkie cannot believe her eyes. Dancing on the dance floor is her ex-fiancé, Walter with a woman that looks familiar to her. The woman looks nice in her cream dress. The more she stares at that woman's face the more she thinks she knows her. It's something about the way she smiles. Then it hits her. No it can't be who I think it is? That means she would have lost over 100 pounds since our high school graduation, Twinkie thinks.

As much as I want to get up and see if that's the woman I think she is, I am not going anywhere near my ex-fiancé and her without my husband. My husband, Hershey is a real man, who treats me like a princess not like dirt. Hershey encourages me and does not put me down or mess with my mind. Hershey did not make a pass at my sister and my cousin like Walter did during our wedding rehearsal dinner. Nor has Hershey hit me one time in all the years we have been married. No, I'll wait until my Hershey gets back from the restroom. I want to warn this woman if Walter has not changed, Twinkie thinks.

Twinkie watches which table Walter and the woman go to. I see Rosita and Wendy over there. Twinkie keeps her eyes focused on that table. Hershey walks back to their table. Twinkie does not even notice him sitting down. Hershey knows his wife. Something is wrong because she has a worried look on her face. Slowly, Hershey reaches over and rubs Twinkie's shoulder. She jumps. Now I really know something is wrong, thinks Hershey.

"Baby, what's wrong?" asks Hershey.

"Walter is here with a woman I graduated from high school with. Oh Sugar, I believe I should warn her about him. But she looks so happy with him. I wanted to go up to her while she was in his arms and tell her every dirty thing he did to me. I don't want anyone going through what I went through. And if she's the woman I think she is, she's been through enough already," says Twinkie.

"What can we do if she's not ready to hear what happened to you?" asks Hershey.

"I'd feel better if I told her regardless of whether she receives it or not. This may be the reason why we're here. Remember I wasn't going to come. I said we could make the next reunion and go on vacation instead. God said, 'Go and have a good time.'

"The woman, who told me Walter was not right for me, walked up to me in the restroom in the restaurant. She heard Walter talking to me as she was sitting a few tables away from us. She admonished me to watch and see what Walter did and did not do. She also told me that Walter was watching other women even while I was in his presence. That woman loved me even when I didn't believe what she was saying. I thought the woman was jealous because I had a man and she was alone.

"I remembered every word that woman said when my cousin and my sister came to me after our wedding rehearsal dinner party. Walter always told me just because we were getting married didn't mean he couldn't look at other women. Yet, Walter didn't want me looking at other men. Walter hit me whenever a man looked at me or talked to me. I thought he would change after we got married. I realized that what the woman said was true after I listened to my cousin and my sister," says Twinkie.

"I understood it more when I met you and you treated me with such kindness, tenderness and love. It was like a miracle walked into my life and I was in heaven. Then you asked me to marry you and we were abstinent during our engagement while you courted me. I don't care if she doesn't receive it. At least she would have heard me and maybe she'll remember it in just enough time to call everything off. Sugar will you go over there with me to talk with her please?" asks Twinkie.

Just then they announced:

"Time for the Dance Contest."

Hershey looks Twinkie directly in her eyes and says:

"You ignore Walter for now. I mean it Sweetheart! Now where's my smile I always see on your face?" Twinkie turns, looks into her husband eyes and smiles.

"Now that's my girl. There's that beautiful smile I always love to see on your face. We'll talk with her Baby right after we win this dance contest. You know I've been practicing my moves. I think we're going to win tonight," says Hershey.

"I agree with you, Sugar on that in Jesus name amen," says Twinkie as the two of them ascend to the dance floor. Other couples approach the dance floor from all over the room. Couples form two lines facing each other with each partner opposite one another and moving to the beat. Partners come and spotlight dance together at the beginning of the two lines down through the center of the two moving lines of people until the end of the lines. After couples finish their spotlight dancing, they fall back in their respective places at the end of the two lines so another couple can spotlight dance down the middle of the two moving lines. The reunion committee requested three unbiased people from the restaurant staff be judges. Brandon grabs Roberta's arm and says,

"Let's do this Baby! We're going to win!"

"Not if Florence and I are on the dance floor! We're the best dancers here! Come on Florence let's show them how it's really done," says Walter.

"The judges tell you, who the best dancers are. And it will be us! I've been dancing since I was an infant. Nobody has moves like I do. Watch gentlemen and weep when Camellita and I win the prize," says Jeremiah.

The couples leave the table and go to the dance floor. Percy looks at Wendy and asks,

"Do you dance? I know some Christians don't dance to this music at all."

"Yes, I do. But I only dance with people, who ask me to dance," says Wendy.

"Well alright now. Make me work for it. Okay! Will you dance with me Wendy?" asks Percy.

"I believe I will. Thank you for asking me Percy," says Wendy.

"Maybe you two will win that prize and Jeremiah will be left with egg on his face," says Rosita.

The three laugh as Percy and Wendy walk away from the table to the dance floor. Rosita gets up to get a better view of the dancers. Standing along the sidelines, a man approaches her. Looking her up and down, he says,

"Rosita Lee!"

"Yes, who are you?" asks Rosita.

"Don't you recognize me? I used to be in your honors biology class. Are you sure you don't recognize me?" He asks.

Rosita looks closely at the man. He looks familiar just like Florence did. Lord, who is this man? Rosita thinks in her mind. Then she hears God. No it can't be him! But God is never wrong! He was darker in high school and rounder. But his features are just like Jerred's. Then Rosita says out loud,

"Jerred?"

"Yes it is I in the flesh," says Jerred.

"You grew taller and got lighter in complexion?" asks Rosita.

"I grew taller in college just like Percy did. The lighter complexion thing is something that happens in my family as the males grow into adulthood," says Jerred.

The announcement comes across the intercom:

"Last call for those participating in the Dance Contest!"

"Do you dance, Rosita?" asks Jerred.

"Yes I do," says Rosita.

"Will you dance with me for the contest?" asks Jerred.

"Yes let's do this and win," says Rosita.

On the dance floor, Twinkie opposite Hershey dances in the lines next to Rosita opposite Jerred. Walter and Florence are really working it as they come down the middle of the lines dancing together. The judges ask the hotel manager to join them in judging the contest. The hotel manager is more familiar with the dance moves than they are.

Walter watches as Jeremiah and Camellita come through the middle of the lines. They can dance! Jeremiah flips, spins around, then grabs Camellita's hands and pulls her through his legs. They have some moves. Percy and Wendy are working it out. This is some high competition, thinks Walter.

Just as Walter begins to relax and thinks he and Florence have this competition, he sees his ex-fiancée: Twinkie dancing next to Rosita. Twinkie looks fine! Does she recognize me? Of course she recognizes me! How could she not? How did I let that fine one get away from me?

Well, I'm not letting Florence get away. She's mine forever, thinks Walter.

As couples are eliminated, the dance competition comes down to three couples:

- Camellita and Jeremiah
- Florence and Walter
- Twinkie and Hershey

People line up to cheer them on and open up the space for them to have plenty of room to do their dance moves. The judges grant these couples five minutes to discuss their dance plans. Many thoughts raced through their minds as they walk to the side to discuss their final moves for the contest to win. The three couples talk over their strategies at three different parts of the dance floor.

I am so glad I wore my sharp knee-length, red after-five-dress, thinks Camellita. Jeremiah thinks about which moves would cinch them winning. I'm so glad I wore my loose black, dress suit. Losing those extra 10 pounds helps me, thinks Jeremiah.

Walter is sweating. This is some stiff competition! Look at Florence. She is not even sweating. What's up with that? Is she even trying??? Florence better be doing her best because she knows how I hate to lose anything, thinks Walter.

And what's up with my ex: Twinkie??? Maybe she recognizes I got someone better than her to take care of me. As a matter of fact come to think of it, Twinkie was slacking in her duties of keeping me happy. After all I did for her, why is she acting like she don't even know me? Twinkie knows I was the best thing that happened to her. That new guy with her, don't even look as good as me. Huh, Twinkie must want me and can't bear to look at me with someone else. I bet he can't handle Twinkie and she needs someone like me on the side ines. Now I know I can handle both her and Florence if Twinkie wants to come back to me, thinks Walter.

Wow, look at us. When I was in nigh school and they had these competitions, no one would dance with me. Now look: a man, my man, my fiancé dancing with me! And we are one of the last three couples to win the prize. Oh, my poor baby is sweating. I'm not sweating. This has been less than 40 minutes and I don't start sweating until I am exercising consistently over an hour. Oh well, he should have come to practice with me this last month like he said he would at least three times a week. Florence thinks.

I have a couple of suggestions I remember from high school that might give us the edge to win if no one else tries the same moves. I'll tell Walter when we talk up close. I don't want anyone to hear our plans and spoil our surprise, thinks Florence.

We're gonna win! We're gonna win! This I know. Walter does not do well under pressure. That is Florence!! She looks good and has been keeping up very well. All those dance classes in high school did Florence some good. Knowing Walter is here in the same building still "creeps me out." I hope Walter does not come near me. Yet, I don't want to be Florence when she and Walter lose. Twinkie thinks.

Camellita and her guy are good. Yet, I still believe Hershey and I are gonna win. Hershey and I just need the best dance strategy to cinch the prize. I wonder: what the prize is? Twinkie thinks.

I saw that Walter looking at my wife, Twinkie. He had better not try anything with her. I'm glad Twinkie's ignoring him like I told her to do so she can enjoy herself. It took a long time to get my wife to trust me even when she became my fiancée. I'm so glad he lost Twinkie because now she's mine. Twinkie is such a precious jewel God has given me. Twinkie is a good name for her since she sparkles whenever she smiles. I love Twinkie so much! Thank you God for my wife, thinks Hershey.

The couples whisper in each other's ear. Florence repeats her suggestion a few times before Walter understands. They don't have time to come up with a plan "B" because Walter seems distracted. Why is Walter staring at that other couple? Florence thinks. To pump her man up, Florence says,

"Baby, you know we can do this. I'm with you. I know how you don't like to lose so I'm giving it my 110%. What about you?" asks Florence.

Walter snaps out of his glazed stare and focuses on Florence. Then he says,

"Yeah Baby, you know me. I can do anything. You're right. We can do this."

In another corner, Hershey pumps up his Twinkie.

"Now Babe, I know we can do this. Don't think about anything else except having fun doing it. Remember how we won that other dance contest? You relaxed, had fun, and realized it was only a contest. Once you remembered that I love you whether we win or lose; we won the contest. If we lose, we'll try again next time. I'm not going to get upset with you or hurt you if we lose," says Hershey.

"Okay," says Twinkie.

"I'm just going to have fun with it," says Twinkie.

In the last corner are Jeremiah and Camellita. Jeremiah speaks first.

"Camellita, we used most of the moves we practiced for the other competitions. Can you think of anything else we can do that will get us ahead?" asks Jeremiah.

Camellita closes her eyes and focuses for a moment. Then it comes to her. There was a move that won a dance competition when she was in high school. Opening her eyes, Camellita explains the move to Jeremiah and asks him how can they add a variation to that dance move? Jeremiah comes up with the answer and shares it right before the judges say "time for them to finish the competition." Camellita agrees with the plan.

The three couples approach the beginning of the dance lines formed by other couples. The music beats fast. The two lines move to the beat. The judges decide the order each couple dances down the lines. This is the last chance to win the prize.

Camellita and Jeremiah are first. Jeremiah flips to a standing position while Camellita dances in place. Next, Jeremiah dances back to where Camellita is. She receives his hand and he spins her around himself down the two lines. The two dance in unison for about four couples down. Jeremiah spins Camellita around himself again. Stopping Camellita behind himself; she bends forward and he pulls her through his legs. The two dance in unity again for about four more couples down.

Jeremiah squats. Ignoring her dress, Camellita puts her hands on Jeremiah's back, spreads her legs and jumps over him like a frog jump she learned in dance class. Jeremiah grabs her hand and they dance in unison until they get to the end of the two lines. The applause is thunderous.

Twinkie and Hershey are second. They start out

dancing in unison in place from the beginning of the lines to the fourth couple down the lines. Next, hand in hand they flip together to a perfect stand in place. The crowd goes wild with cheers. Hershey twirls Twinkie around him about three times. They do one of the Preston High School cheers that Twinkie taught Hershey. They stop in the middle, cartwheel in unity together and both of them perform a perfect split almost at the end of the lines. Getting up in unison they kiss and move to the music to the end of the lines. There is a thunderous applause from those in the lines and those at the tables watching.

Florence and Walter are last. No one is talking. You can hear only the music playing. The people from the kitchen came out to watch the last three couples compete. People walking in the hallway hearing the music and the crowd, stepped inside the ballroom to view the competition as well.

Walter has beads of sweat popping out on his forehead and flowing down his back. This is some heavy competition! And they just did the move we're going to do! My girl is right! We can do this. We better be better than them. I'll make a few changes, thinks Walter.

Whispering in Florence's ear as they come together, Walter says,

"Follow my lead."

Florence grimaces. Anytime Walter says "follow his lead," he is about to mess up. Watching Walter closely, they start just like the previous couple. They both do a flip together in unison. As they come to a perfect stand, Walter twirls Florence around himself twice. So far so good, thinks Florence. If he can only remember the other cheer I taught him, thinks Florence.

As they start doing the cheer, Walter's mind draws a blank. He starts the cheer and Florence finishes the cheer. The crowd completes the cheer with Florence in unison. It's okay Florence thinks because sometimes they did that cheer in high school that way where one person started the cheer and the other person finished it.

She sees the look in Walter's eyes. Next, they do a cartwheel together then a split in unison. Rising together they come to a perfect stand. Walter twirls her around himself two more times. To compete with the other couples' performance Walter shouts to Florence, "One more flip!" Florence completes her flip but Walter does not. In fact, Walter falls on his butt.

"Oh, my god!" Someone gasps.

"Is he okay?" Someone else asks.

Florence continues dancing. Walter gets up and dances in place. Instead of kissing Florence like he was supposed do Walter goes to the end of a line. Tears form in Florence's eyes and slowly trickle down Florence's cheeks. She knows Walter is angry and does not want to get anywhere near him at that moment.

The judges write down their scores. A member of the reunion committee reads the paper and says:

"Will the three couples come forward please?"

The three couples line up next to each other in front of the judges table. The announcement is made over the microphone.

"Runner ups are: **Walter and Florence! They win a $50 gift card!**" The audience applauds them. Walter wraps his arm violently around Florence at her waist as they bow together.

"First place goes to: **Jeremiah and Camellita! They**

win a $100 gift card!" Jeremiah and Camellita grasp hands together and bow at their waists.

"And our winners for the **Dance Competition** this evening are: **Hershey and Twinkie! They win an all-expense paid, three-day-vacation to Florida!**"

Twinkie jumps up and down. Then she kisses Hershey passionately on his lips. Hershey responds then gently wraps his arm around his wife's waist.

"**We did it!**" shouts Twinkie.

As the envelope is handed to them, Twinkie gives it to Hershey for safe keeping. Next Twinkie shouts:

"**Thank you! Thank you so much! Oh my, we appreciate this! We can and will use this right away! Thank you Jesus!**"

Next Twinkie whispers in Hershey's ear.

"Look at God! I obeyed Him to come here tonight and He paid for our vacation for us! We don't have to spend our money. He knows I wanted to go to Florida. God is faithful! God is good!" says Twinkie.

"Yes He is," says Hershey as he smiles and nods his head.

Walter mumbles under his breath. He is worried about what people are thinking and will say. Florence stands perfectly still not knowing what to do with Walter's arm firmly planted around her waist. She does not move so she won't trigger Walter's anger any further. Florence does not even ask Walter: what is he saying?

Standing close by are: Rosita, Wendy, Jerred and Percy. Watching every move Walter makes, they notice how tightly he is holding onto Florence. Wendy, Rosita and Percy pray softly under their breath. Jerred realizing what they are doing joins in. Rosita's eyes widen as she realizes Jerred joined the three of them in prayer. Jerred moves out towards Walter first. Rosita follows him.

"Man: Walter I didn't know you would be here tonight! Last time I saw you, was at the fitness center on 117th street in Chicago. I didn't know that was the reason you were working out. Man those are some great moves you have! Congratulations, you beat out Brandon and Roberta. With all the bragging they do I'm glad you made it into the top three and not them. I would have heard it here and all over social media. That's good enough for me. Man, you were really moving," says Jerred.

Walter calms down with the attention focused on him and the accolades for his effort.

"Yeah Man it's good to see you. You know Florence, my fiancé?" asks Walter.

"Florence: that is you! Girl you look good! You lost a lot of weight. You're better than me," says Jerred patting his belly.

"The two of you on the dance floor move good together. Too bad I can't dance like you. I was dancing with Rosita and we were eliminated the first round," says Jerred.

Wendy and Percy continue praying softly. Although talking with other couples a distance away, Twinkie and Hershey face Walter and Florence to watch for an opportunity to talk with Florence.

"Man you know, we work on these moves from time to time. I was just a little bit rusty tonight," says Walter. He releases his hold on Florence. She puts her hand to her mouth so that her sigh of relief is not heard audibly. Then Florence wipes her eyes and straightens out her clothes.

"Man after all that dancing, you must be thirsty. Do you want to get a soda or something?" asks Jerred.

"Man, you know, I am a bit parched. I think I could use something," says Walter.

"Well, I know I'm thirsty just watching you. Hey Percy, you want to join us for a soda or something? Walter and I are headed for the bar. My treat," says Jerred.

"Yeah, I'm a bit dry myself. Here I come," says Percy.

"Florence: are you coming with us?" asks Walter.

"Man why don't we let the women talk? You know your woman. Let us men do the talking and bring our women a drink back. If that's okay with you Man?" asks Jerred.

"Yeah, we can handle the drinks ourselves. You're right. I'm the man!" says Walter.

Jerred, Percy and Walter walk out towards the bar. Rosita, Wendy and Florence stand there for a second.

"Florence, girl you were working it," says Wendy.

"Thank you. We do practice but Walter did not come to practice for the last three weeks," says Florence.

"I don't know if I could have done that in those shoes and with that cream colored dress on. Girl, you had your moves down good. I need to visit the little girls' room. How about you?" asks Wendy.

"Yes, I would like to freshen up after all that dancing before the men get back," says Florence.

"You coming Rosita?" asks Wendy.

"Yes, I need to freshen up myself," says Rosita.

Watching the three women go to their table and pick up their purses, Twinkie waits to see where Walter is at. Watching what Walter does, she waits to see if he turns around to see where Florence is at just like he used to do her. Twinkie notices Florence is watching Walter's position as well. Twinkie knows all too well that Walter is known for going with the guys then changing his mind if he sees his woman is doing something he doesn't like, like talking with a man or trying to get away.

Walter stops walking and looks back at the three women talking. He follows them with his eyes as they go over to the table, continue talking, pick up their purses and head for the ladies room. "Good they are headed to the ladies room. She can't get away from me there because she has to pass by the bar to get out," thinks Walter.

"Man, Walter are you coming?" asks Jerred as he and Percy stop walking.

Satisfied that Florence is only talking with the women and there are no men around, Walter relaxes.

"Yeah, Man here I come," says Walter. He catches up with the men and they continue forward to the bar in the next room.

Twinkie satisfied that Walter is not going to come back to Florence at that moment, excuses herself from the current conversation she is in. Twinkie winks at Hershey. This is my open door to talk with Florence without Walter knowing, Twinkie thinks to herself. Twinkie picks up her purse from the table she and Hershey are sitting at and heads to the ladies room herself.

Rosita, Wendy and Florence enter the restroom. Florence sits down in one of the chairs, sighs and put her face in her hands. Rosita and Wendy are just about to talk with her, when Twinkie comes into the restroom. Looking around to see if anyone is in any of the stalls, Twinkie goes over to Florence and hugs her. Rosita and Wendy look at each other with puzzled expressions. "Why did she search to see if anyone else is in the ladies room with us?" I'm going to ask her, thinks Rosita. Before she can, Twinkie begins talking.

"Florence girl you look good! I didn't know for sure that was you until I heard the announcement for third place. You guys did a good job and you look great," says Twinkie. She steps back from hugging Florence and sits in one of the chairs.

"Twinkie Davis! I remember you from our history classes. Talking about me looking great! You look great as well! You guys were fantastic on the dance floor. Yet I don't remember you being as flexible in high school?" says Florence.

"You're right. I was afraid in high school to go to the next level. Later I went through a traumatic and dangerous relationship. I was about to get married to the wrong person after I got out of college. I went to counseling with my pastor and his wife. Once I finished that, I looked at my life and put fear out of my life. Everything I was afraid to do: I took classes to conquer any fear and keep all fear out of my life.

"It took me a few years but I finally was ready to get married and God sent the right man for me. Before I tell you about my great husband and our great life, wouldn't you like to know: who I was in a relationship with that was so traumatic and dangerous for me? He's here at this reunion," says Twinkie.

"I want to know so that I don't get involved with the wrong man. I mean you know God can fix a person's heart and they stop doing what they did. But what if that person hasn't changed?" asks Rosita.

"Girl, I'll tell you in minute. But right now, I'm asking Florence **if she wants to know** the person's name?" asks Twinkie.

"I guess I do since that person is here at the reunion.

I don't want to run into someone like that even though I'm in a relationship right now and engaged. Who is it?" asks Florence.

"It's Walter Harris!" says Twinkie.

Chapter 10
The Secret

"My Walter Harris???" asks Florence with a startled look on her face.

Placing one of their hands over their mouths, Rosita and Wendy look at each other. Each of them grabs one of the last two remaining chairs. They sit down. Rosita prays softly. Wendy hearing Rosita praying follows Rosita's lead and prays softly as well. This is God! It wasn't for me to talk with Florence. It was for me to pray for the person talking with Florence, thinks Rosita.

God is good! Wendy thinks. Here Rosita was trying to figure out a way to get Florence's attention without hurting her feelings and God uses Twinkie from high school to talk with Florence. There is nobody like you God, thinks Wendy.

So many thoughts flood Florence's mind. Walter and Twinkie engaged? Wow! He never told me about her? Walter did say that he was engaged to someone else but he never said who that person was? Why was it so dangerous and traumatic for Twinkie? Florence thinks.

"No you must be mistaken, Twinkie. Walter is a kind and sweet man. Why would it be dangerous and traumatic for you to be with Walter?" asks Florence.

"Oh it was Walter all right. I'll tell you my story and let you decide for yourself. Ladies before I proceed, this is my secret I'm about to tell you. My husband knows bits and pieces but not the entire story. Please don't share this with anyone else," says Twinkie.

Rosita, Wendy and Florence nod their heads indicating "yes." Twinkie proceeds with her secret.

"I had just come out of an aerobics class from the fitness

club in the south suburbs of Chicago on 123rd and Cicero. This man walks up to me and starts flirting with me. I smile and I don't think anything further of it. The next time I come to class, he is in the aerobics class with me keeping up with me as I exercise. When I go to my spinning class, the man is there too. At first, I think he's stalking me. I should have followed that thought and stuck with that thought. Well, when it came time for me to pay my next monthly bill, the manager tells me my bill has already been paid. Not only has next month's bill been paid but the bill was paid in full for the next three months.

"Now I feel obligated to say 'thank you' to the person, who paid my bill for three months. I asked the manager, who paid my bill and how did he get my name? The manager said the man pointed me out to him. He told the manager he wanted to pay my bill for three months. The manager said he would not give the man my name because of my privacy rights but the man left his card in case I wanted to get in touch with him. The manager told me that the man still did not know my name," says Twinkie.

"I asked the manager which man was it and if the man was there that night? The manager directed me to a man working out on a bench over in the corner. That man was the same man, who flirted with me that time outside the building and was in my classes. I walked over to where that man was working out and introduced myself to him.

"He told me his name was Walter Harris. I thanked the man for his generosity. He asked me out to dinner. I told him I appreciated his offer and I declined. I was very impressed that he took the rejection so well. I switched my hips as I walked away from him. If you know that place, there are mirrors all over. I saw the other guys go up to him as I switched walking away and I saw Walter's face. He had this huge grin on his face as he watched me walk away," says Twinkie.

"When Walter paid my bill again for my next three months at the fitness center, I gave him my number and agreed to go out to dinner with him but I would meet him there. Walter was such a gentleman. He opened doors. He didn't pressure me to sleep with him. He brought me flowers. He paid for dinner every time we went out. I finally introduced him to my family.

"Let me share a few things about Walter that may sound familiar to you," says Twinkie. She talks fast and everyone has to keep up. She desires to get her point across as quickly as possible. Twinkie changes the subject whenever someone walks in the restroom. She doesn't want anyone hear her secret or Florence's business.

Florence's demeanor slowly changes while Twinkie talks. Florence focuses on what Twinkie has said when other women enter the restroom and Twinkie changes the subject. Florence realizes, "I met Walter the same way Twinkie described but at a different center. First Walter paid my fitness bill for a month. I said 'thank you' to him as well. Next we introduced ourselves to each other," thinks Florence.

After that introduction I still wouldn't go out with him, even though he attended the same classes I did. I finally agreed to go out with Walter after he paid my fitness bill in advance for four months! To me it was the least thing I could do for Walter's kindness, Florence thinks.

I know Walter all too well, thinks Twinkie. One time, Walter came into the women's restroom in a restaurant when I took too long to come out. When Walter entered the restroom, someone screamed! It was so embarrassing! The woman, who screamed told the restaurant owner. The owner asked Walter and me to leave. Walter really beat me that night because he was embarrassed for being put out of that restaurant **after he came in the women's restroom after me**, thinks Twinkie.

Twinkie, Rosita and Wendy talk about fashion designs while other women are in the restroom. Florence keeps quiet pondering her first encounters with Walter.

We started dating on a regular basis after that. About two months later, I took Walter to one of my family events. Four months later he proposed marriage to me at a second family event right in front of all my relatives. Walter had a ring and got down on one knee. Florence thinks.

I was surprised. All my family except my sister and my college girlfriend thought it was so romantic! I thought they were being haters. I said "Yes," and Walter put the ring on my finger. We kissed and everyone clapped. I'm wearing the ring on my finger right now, Florence thinks.

It's not something I imagined I'd wear since I like yellow gold and diamonds for a ring. But this is so unusual as it is a light blue sapphire stone with petite diamonds surrounding it on white gold. Walter said he liked the light blue sapphire so much and he thought of me when he saw it. That's why Walter got this one for me. It's so special that Walter thought about me when he brought this engagement ring, Florence thinks.

The last woman finally finishes washing her hands while the four women sit. That woman exits the restroom. Twinkie walks over to the door and looks out to see if anyone else is coming. Good no one else is coming, Twinkie thinks. Walking back to the sink, Twinkie grabs the "out of order sign" from under the sink, walks back to the door, puts it on the outside of the door, closes the door and locks it from the inside. This is too important for any further interruptions since Florence's life could be at stake, thinks Twinkie.

"Twinkie what are you doing?" asks Florence. Rosita and Wendy look on with bated breath and wait to hear what Twinkie's response is.

"There's another bigger women's restroom closer to the bar. I need to finish this before my husband comes looking for me if that's okay with you Florence?" asks Twinkie.

"Oh okay," says Florence.

Twinkie thinks "good." I'm glad she accepted that answer. I wasn't sure what else I was going to say, thinks Twinkie. Rosita closes her eyes briefly and lets out a cleansing breath. Wendy digs in her purse for something and whispers "thank you Jesus."

Twinkie continues with her story. Rosita and Wendy continue praying very softly while they all listen to Twinkie. She tells the three women how everything was going well. She and Walter were together so much and he was so sweet to her that Twinkie agreed to move out of her apartment into Walter's condo. Twinkie's family was totally against her living with Walter and did not hold back their opinions whenever Twinkie and Walter were around them.

Walter asked Twinkie when they were lying in the bed one night, what was her favorite stone? Twinkie told Walter she liked light blue sapphire. One night at a dinner party with all Walter's friends around, Walter got down on one knee and pulled out a pretty light blue sapphire ring with small petite diamonds surrounding the stone on white gold. The ring was so beautiful. Walter asked Twinkie to marry him right there in front of all his friends. She said, "Yes." They kissed and danced the rest of the night.

"When I told my family, they were ecstatic except my sister and my cousin. I couldn't understand why? Although I was in love with Walter and after I agreed to marry Walter, some things were still not right," says Twinkie.

Florence looks at the ring on her finger. Shaking her head in unbelief, she twists the ring around her finger. Florence looks directly into Twinkie's face, raises her right hand and asks,

"Is this the ring?"

Twinkie nods her head indicating "yes." Tears stream down Florence's face. Wendy pushes her chair closer to Florence and puts her arm around Florence while Florence cries. No one says anything but Twinkie as she continues her story.

"Walter became very possessive. If a man looked at me, Walter accused me of thinking of leaving him to be with that man. One night we were at a club, Walter got too drunk. When he saw a man was looking at my behind, Walter got into a fight with that man. The man beat Walter really bad. I was shocked. I had never seen Walter behave like that. It scared me a little.

"Once I got home with Walter things got worse. Although Walter had bruises and wounds from the fight, Walter was angry with me! He blamed me for him getting into a fight with that man. He said I provoked the man by what I was wearing. When I told Walter it wasn't my fault, he slapped me hard in my face. Then Walter tore my dress off of my body. He said, 'no one will ever look at me like that man did again!' It was my precious $250 dress I got on sale for $75! I tried to defend myself but Walter was stronger. He sat on me, pinned my hands above my head and slapped me in my face repeatedly. I screamed and cried but no one came to my rescue," says Twinkie.

"He finally got off of me, picked me up from the floor and held me close to him. Walter apologized by saying he was sorry. He told me 'I made him act like that' because he loved me so much that he couldn't stand to watch another man looking at me. Walter walked me to our bedroom. We had sex then he went to sleep with his arm around my waist.

"I couldn't get his arm off of me no matter how hard I tried. He felt like dead weight. Finally Walter moved and I grabbed my purse, eased off the bed and ran towards the bedroom door. He jumped out of the bed, grabbed my purse, dumped out its contents, took my cell phone, mashed it, grabbed me, threw me back on the bed, and told me I wasn't going anywhere," says Twinkie.

"I told him I had to go to the bathroom. Walter walked me to the bathroom, watched me pee, wash my hands and look at myself in the mirror. Tears ran down my face when I saw how swollen my face was and that one eye was purplish.

"Walter wrapped his arms around my waist, kissed me all over my neck, told me he was sorry and it wouldn't happen again. Walter asked me: if I believed him? I said 'yes' out of fear. Walter then picked me up, carried me to bed and had sex with me again. He fell into a deep sleep this time but had his leg and his arm wrapped over my body. I could not get out from under his grip. When I awoke in the morning, he was not beside me in the bed. I got up and looked in the mirror. One eye was completely shut. Walter left a note that he was sorry and it wouldn't happen again," says Twinkie.

"When I walked through the condo, Walter was sitting in the living room. He scared me. When I started backing up from him, he talked to me softly. He had fixed breakfast. He called my job saying I wasn't feeling well and would not be in that day. Walter then called his job and told them he would work from home that day.

"I was so scared that I agreed to do whatever Walter said. I had never been treated like that. Walter promised it wouldn't happen again. He put raw potato on my eye and held me most of the next three days I wasn't allowed to dress in anything other than a night grown. To escape him, I pretended to be sleep several times. About the third day, I finally stopped trembling whenever Walter walked into a room," says Twinkie.

"Walter worked from home for that week and the next week. To apologize, Walter purchased all types of fresh flowers daily. He made every meal and fed me himself. I went back to work on the fourth day of the first week with plenty of makeup on my face to hide my injuries. Walter drove me to work, met me for lunch, and picked me up after work. He did that for the end of that week and the following week. Walter also called me on my job every hour and a half to say he was sorry.

"He sounded like he meant what he said. Walter gave back the keys to my car and told me that we had the same navigational device on our cars. He wanted me to have the most up-to-date model like his. Walter sounded like his old self and I believed it would not happen again," says Twinkie.

"There was a death in my family. Walter couldn't go with me because of his job. He was working on a big deal that would land him a huge bonus. Walter insisted I take my car. Mama told Walter they were taking only one car and I was riding with Daddy and her. That way the three of us could share the driving to Carlinville, IL. That's when Walter started working on my mind.

"Walter stated things like: 'no man will ever want you but me.' Another thing he said was: 'I'd better not be looking at or talking with any other man. If I did, he would know about it.' There were so many degrading things Walter said to me that I was afraid to talk with anyone about it. The one thing I can remember that really scared me is Walter said he would hurt my parents if I didn't come back to him," says Twinkie.

Twinkie looks at her watch and realizes they have been in the restroom about 20 minutes. To make sure that she gets her final points across, Twinkie switches gears. She says,

"For the sake of time I'm going to shorten this up. Something happened to Mama and Daddy's car. They put it in the shop and couldn't get it out in time for the trip. We had to use my car. Walter was ecstatic. He filled up my car with gas for the trip, gave me money for gas for the entire trip and watched us leave. Walter was smiling so hard, I thought it was strange.

"When we got to Carlinville, we had a tire blow out. The family mechanic changed the tire and checked out the spare. We left my car with him to check out the rest of the car to make sure there was nothing else wrong. We rode around with other family members. After the funeral and before we went to pick up my car, the mechanic, who used to date my sister, came by our family's house with some alarming news," says Twinkie.

"A tracking system and a water-proof tape recorder

were under the hood recording everything spoken inside my car and within a five foot parameter surrounding the outside of my car. The tracking device was a state-of-the-art system that monitored and transmitted the mileage traveled, direction of the car, weight and height of each passenger; and any deviation from the route. And, yes! The route from Chicago to Carlinville, IL and back was programmed into this device with the expected mileage marked. The device was set to transmit immediately any deviation from that mileage or route programmed into it," says Twinkie.

Rosita, Florence and Wendy gasp with shock.

"I realized then what he said about knowing if I was talking with any man. It would be because he had the tape recorder to listen to. I was really grateful that we only asked the mechanic to change the tire when we were standing close up on the car. We did not ask him to look over the rest of the car until after we went into the main office, used the restroom facilities and stood in the lounge area talking about old times. So the part about the mechanic looking over the rest of the car was not on the recorder hidden under the car hood. The mechanic also gave my parents a copy of what was on the tape recorder.

"I knew I had to go back to Walter if for nothing else but to keep my parents alive. But I was really scared! Walter had followed me on various occasions to make sure I was where I said I was going. Although he promised he would not beat me again, Walter beat me several times over the stress of his job and other things that he accused me of. He said these things were my fault that they happened. Walter always apologized with flowers and said it wouldn't happen again," says Twinkie.

"My parents rode back with me and I asked them not to say anything to Walter about it. They agreed but told me inside the house that they would stop by and have my siblings, uncles and cousins stop by periodically to check up on me. I was glad I hadn't said anything derogatory about Walter on the way there. On the way home, we played music and barely spoke so that nothing else would be recorded on the tape recorder.

"When I got home, Walter was ecstatic to see us. He took my car to the shop to make sure nothing was wrong with it and that the mechanic didn't do anything to my car. I understood why. Walter was checking on the tape recorder and the tracking device," says Twinkie.

"For the fourth time I lied to keep from getting a beating. I told Walter that the mechanic only changed the tire and reconditioned the spare nothing else. Mama and Daddy told me to make sure that's all I told Walter when he brought it up. And they were right, Walter did bring it up.

"Three things happened that finally helped me to see I was in a traumatic and dangerous situation. Number one, I found someone else's underwear under the mattress when I changed the sheets. I also was missing a white work blouse that went with my suit. I always set up my clothes together so that when I am ready to wear any particular suit, the appropriate blouse would be right there next to it. My white blouse was gone. While I was too afraid to ask Walter about the underwear, I did ask him about my white blouse. He told me to check his closet because the cleaning lady might have mixed them up. I let it go as I had already done that," says Twinkie.

"Number two was I got beaten worse and worse every time we lost a dance competition. You remember how I used to love to dance in high school? Well, we took classes together and were really good if we stayed on track with the routine we practiced. Walter bragged with his friends about what a good dance couple we were and took bets on the side. If we lost and he lost money, it was always my fault even if he fell like he did tonight. Some kind of way Walter's ego got in the competition. Walter would say: 'Follow my lead.' When I realized Walter changed the steps, I associated that with the beating I would get when we got home when we lost. I then tried to get out of dancing with him. Once Walter released me from dancing because I faked being sick to keep from dancing. I thank God it worked and we did not dance that night. The couple, who won was really good and I knew we could not beat them.

"I lost my desire to dance after that and took up playing the piano. Something Walter had no interest in. Every now and then, whenever I thought of dancing competitively; my body shook violently. Because whenever we lost no matter why we lost, Walter blamed me for our failure, berated me mentally, beat me physically, had sex with me to make sure I knew he was in control and took me to work the next day. Walter also sent flowers to my job saying he was sorry and expected to see those flowers on my desk when he picked me up from work that night," says Twinkie.

"Number three: Walter made passes at my sister and my cousin at our wedding rehearsal dinner party. He told my sister that he couldn't wait until I was married to him so that he, Walter could be the rooster over her and me. They both told me in the restroom of the hotel. I had had enough.

"I decided to talk with Daddy, Mama, my sister and my cousins. I told them everything that had happened to me. I also told them how Walter threatened to kill Mama and Daddy if I left him. I told them at that point I was not in love with Walter. I told them I was really scared of Walter. I didn't want to marry Walter and wanted to move as far away as I could from Walter," says Twinkie.

"My family devised a plan. While Walter was at his bachelor party getting drunk in the Royal Banquet Hall of the hotel; two of my male cousins stayed there keeping an eye on Walter. My four other male cousins went with my sister, my female cousins, my aunties and my best friends to the condo. They packed up all my belongings, moved them out of the condo and stored them in one of my uncle's second houses in Crete, IL.

"They also went to the hotel rooms we were staying in and removed all of my things including my wedding dress. We had adjoining rooms. I was to lock mine once it was our actual wedding day. I gave them the room key and the ring before they got started. They left it on the night stand in Walter's room for him to see," says Twinkie.

"My other uncle knew a good mechanic that understood the latest things in technology. They removed all the tracking devices from my car. Then my uncle John put my car in his garage and gave me his second car to use.

"Mama and Daddy went with me to the hospital as I had fresh bruises on my body I covered up with makeup. I finally admitted: I needed help. I told the doctor my fiancé beat me the night previously because a man whistled at me while we were walking down the street together. The doctor took x-rays and ultra-sounds of my body. He saw where I had a broken rib, a previously fractured arm and other bruises that only appear via testing. He recommended several women's abuse shelters for me to go to. The doctor provided copies of the x-rays and his findings so that I could get a restraining order against Walter the next day," says Twinkie.

"My cousins assigned to watch Walter after the bachelor's party ended, deposited his drunk behind in his room and put the 'Do not Disturb' sign on the door. They unplugged the alarm clock, phones, and television in the room. They made sure that his cell phone was on silent; turned off all his alarms on his cell phone; deleted all my family's names and numbers from his cell phone; checked his handheld tablet personal computer to see what was on it; erased the tracking system on it; deleted all my family's names and numbers from it; removed the back of his handheld tablet personal computer so that it would not work; put the cell phone next to the wedding ring on the night stand; and left the room.

"Since the wedding was not scheduled until five o'clock that evening and the bride is not expected to see the groom that day; this was the best time to take action. Mama spoke with her pastor and told him the wedding was off. My family and friends quietly left the hotel one-by-one," says Twinkie.

"To make sure no one suspected anything, most of my family took their luggage to their cars first. They retrieved their gifts from the Kingdom Banquet Hall, where we were to get married. They checked out of the hotel and went to local family members' homes to rest for their return trips home. They did not want be there when the rest of Walter's family and friends arrived for the wedding.

"The plan was if any of Walter's family saw them and asked why they were leaving each of them was instructed to say: a family emergency came up that had to be attended to right away. A few of my cousins, who like drama, remained for the duration of their original hotel stay to enjoy the spa treatments and pool. These cousins waited around to see what Walter and his family would do. Since most of Walter's family was in their respective rooms when my family left, no one asked that question. My sister and my cousins took the R.S.V.P. list; called all my friends and other family; and told them the wedding was off," says Twinkie.

"On the planned wedding day, I went to the Markham Courthouse in Markham, IL. Mama, Daddy, and I took out restraining orders there against Walter. My other family members went one-by-one to various courthouses in Cook County, Will County, and Macoupin County in Illinois to get restraining orders against Walter Harris of Chicago, IL.

"I went to my job. I spoke with human resources and our union. I requested my business not be published but respected and kept silent. I asked for an extended leave of absence; picked up paperwork to transfer to a different part of Illinois; changed my cell phone number; and registered into one of those women's shelters. I didn't want Walter to find me at any of my relatives' homes. I wanted to keep my family safe with no trace of where I was," says Twinkie.

"For the first time in a long time, I slept through the night peacefully with no fear. There I received counseling, medical care, and eventually Jesus in my heart.

"My cousins, who stayed reported to my family and me. Walter finally woke up after his family banged on his hotel room door about five o'clock that night (the time we were to get married). When he showed up at Mama and Daddy's house he was arrested immediately because of the in-place restraining order. Mama and Daddy wouldn't even talk with him. They just called the police, had him arrested and appeared in court," says Twinkie.

"Mama and Daddy produced pictures of my beaten body; copies of the x-rays and results of the testing taken by the doctor with the doctor's certified diagnosis. They told the judge what happened to me and the threats Walter made on their lives to me. The judge gave Walter a three-day sleepover in the Cook County jail without bail and the bailiff put those silver bracelets on Walter. The judge continued the case to have me come to court and testify against Walter.

"When I showed up in court on the day scheduled, I went in with Mama, Daddy, and an attorney. I did not look Walter directly in the eyes except briefly when instructed by my attorney because I knew how Walter could communicate a threat to me. My parents produced that copy of the tape recording found under my car hood the mechanic made for them. Walter told the judge he loved me and wanted me back. The judge reviewed the evidence and admonished Walter to stay away from my family and me," says Twinkie.

"Mama and Daddy got a new alarm system for their house, garage, and on their cars; just in case Walter was crazy enough to come back. And he was! Walter got arrested again. This time the judge gave him 30 days of camp time at the Cook County Jail to cool off with an order to complete anger management classes.

"Walter's attorney requested that something be worked out so he could keep his job. The judge was kind because for those 30 days he let Walter work during the day. Walter had to check in each week night Monday through Thursday at 6:30 p.m. and by 7 p.m. on Friday for the weekend. The program released Walter to work each morning Monday through Friday at 6 a.m. The judge warned Walter if he saw Walter again during those 30 days that there were be no working out anything to keep his job because he would be locked up inside 24/7 for 180 days. The judge spelled it out completely to Walter: 180 days is six months," says Twinkie.

Twinkie finishes by saying,

"Whether you believe it or not: Walter is not a nice man nor does he care about you. Everything he does is for himself. Walter is selfish, immature, angry, self-centered, self-absorbed and full of pride. You make him look good, which is why he chose you. You're a beautiful woman, who deserves the best. You deserve someone, who appreciates you, cherishes you, values your life, and does not hurt you mentally and/or physically. That is who God gave me in my husband: Hershey.

"God has the same for you in someone else, especially since Walter has not changed. I saw the look on your face when you guys ended the dance. You were so terrified that you wouldn't move. I remember that fear because I knew a beating was coming when we either got home or in the car with sex following to prove Walter was the man in control. Do you want to continue in a lifestyle of fear?" asks Twinkie.

Tears flow down Florence's face. Things do not add up for me either, Florence thinks. Yet, this is a lot to hear at one time. I believe Walter loves me. He says it every day. Yet, I'm very afraid to go home tonight, especially if Walter is going beat me when we get home. Florence thinks.

Rosita and Wendy thank God for answering their prayers and the truth coming out about Walter. They continue praying softly.

Twirling the ring around on her finger nervously, Florence says,

"No I don't want a lifestyle of fear. Maybe it won't happen tonight. You don't understand Walter. He's really a kind man. He only gets upset when he's been around his family or my family. We're here tonight away from both of them. We lost a competition last month and he didn't hit me that night. I think Walter has changed from when he was with you.

"I don't like the fact that this was originally your ring designed for you: Twinkie. That means it's not as special to me anymore. All this information about Walter is new to me. I don't think he will go after other women because Walter loves me only," says Florence.

Silence follows Florence's comment. Twinkie, Wendy, and Rosita know that Walter hasn't changed a single bit.

Rosita thinks, **"This woman is in denial!"** I've got to tell her Walter hasn't changed. In fact, Walter made a pass at me tonight, Rosita thinks. Rosita opens her mouth to tell Florence what happened to her this very night and her jaw hurts.

"What is that God?" Rosita whispers softly. Then Rosita hears very clearly, "No, don't say a word." The way the two messages manifest simultaneously lets Rosita know it's a strong "stop" from God. Rosita wants to tell Florence how Walter made a pass at her that very night but doesn't say a word. Rosita trusts God. She and Wendy continue praying softly.

Twinkie listens for God's instructions. She hears from God. Twinkie says,

"I realize all this is hard to hear. We can't help you without God's support and protection. You can't help yourself or see the truth without God's assistance. Do you know Jesus?"

Florence says,

"I believe God exists because He helped me lose weight."

Twinkie says,

"God helps people all the time. Perhaps I should be a little clearer. Have you received The Lord Jesus Christ in your heart? If you did, we can pray that Jesus helps you see the truth. If you haven't, we can introduce you to Jesus. Let Him help you and protect you. Jesus is the one, who loves you not Walter. Jesus wants you in His family."

Just then Florence hears two different voices in her head at the same time. One voice is very soft, steady and clear. It says,

"Jesus loves you very much. He's been waiting a long time to show you how much he cares. There is more Jesus wants to do for you than weight loss. Let them introduce you to Jesus. There is so much more for you. Let them introduce you to Jesus."

The other voice is the familiar voice Florence hears in her head from time to time. It says,

"Have I ever steered you wrong? I showed you how to keep Walter when you couldn't keep that other guy: Quincy. Quincy only liked you for your money and what you brought him."

The familiar voice continues and says,

"Walter pays for everything. Walter takes good care of you. Walter even planned a cruise trip for you two to take. Doesn't Twinkie sound like your teetee Yolanda? Your teetee Yolanda told you Walter wasn't the right one for you in front of Walter. It was so embarrassing. Walter showed her. He surprised you with a weekend getaway two weeks later. Twinkie sounds like your teetee Yolanda."

The soft voice starts again. It says,

"Jesus loves you. There is more for you than weight loss. Jesus wants to be your friend."

The familiar voice gets very loud.

"**Twinkie sounds like your teetee Yolanda**! Look at your watch. You need to go since Walter doesn't know anyone else here. Go spend time with your man, the man I found you. If you do what they're suggesting, they're going to tell everyone your business in one of their testimony services at their church like your family does. **You know you're a private person**! You don't want them putting you on blast like that do you? Twinkie sounds like your teetee Yolanda," says the familiar voice.

Florence looks at her watch.

"Oh my, look at how long we've been in here. I've got to go because Walter doesn't know anyone else here. Could we keep everything said here tonight a secret please? Besides you sound like my teetee Yolanda," says Florence.

Twinkie nods her head. Looking at Rosita and Wendy, Twinkie asks,

"Ladies do you agree that what was said here remains our secret not to be shared with any other human person not even our spouses, friends or fiancés?"

Wendy and Rosita say in unison,

"Agreed."

Twinkie reaches into her purse and pulls out a card. When she does that, Rosita and Wendy search their purses for their cards. All three women give Florence their cards. Twinkie says,

"Here's my cell number. Let's keep in touch. Maybe we can go out to lunch sometime then I'll get to tell you all about how I met my wonderful husband. I'd like to get to know you as an adult, if it's okay with you? And if you ever desire to talk, call me any time. I can be a quiet listening, non-judging ear just letting you talk." Twinkie gives Florence a hug. Rosita stands.

"That's my cell and office number there. That's a good idea. Girl I double that: let's all do lunch! Maybe it could be next month. But I do wanna keep in touch also. May I have your telephone number please? I love you, Florence," says Rosita as she hugs Florence.

Florence gives Rosita her cell phone number. Rosita puts it in her cell phone right then. Twinkie asks Florence,

"Is it okay for me to have your cell number too?"

"Yes, you all may have it," says Florence.

Both Twinkie and Wendy put Florence's cell number in their own cell phones. Wendy stands and touches her business card that she gave Florence.

Wendy says,

"Oh Girl just call me: anytime, at any one of these numbers. Let's talk like we used to, okay?" Hugging Florence deeply, Wendy whispers in her ear;

"You know I love you!"

Florence nods her head, wipes tears from her eyes, corrects her makeup, grabs her purse, unlocks the door and exits the restroom. Twinkie gets up and locks the door once more. The three women sit back down in the chairs.

"Ladies let us pray for Florence right now. Walter hasn't changed one bit and she's in denial. We promised to keep everything spoken a secret and not share it with any human person. We're going to do that," says Twinkie.

"We all know that Jesus is God and man. So we're going to talk with the God: Jesus. We're going to ask God to shut the mouth of the enemy, protect her from death, open her eyes, draw her to God, help her to receive Jesus in her heart, find her a church home, help her to leave Walter until he gets right with God or God gives her a better man; and that Florence receives the good life God has for her. If that's okay with you two ladies and you agree?" asks Twinkie.

Wendy and Rosita nod their heads indicating "yes." The three ladies hold hands together and pray for Florence. When the ladies finish praying, they hug each other. After they exchange cards amongst themselves, Twinkie unlocks the door, removes the sign, places it where she found it, and looks at herself in the mirror. Wendy and Rosita look in the mirror too. They all laugh loudly.

"You didn't know this but streaky mascara, darkened eyes and smudged makeup from tears on our faces are how Rosita and I found our way to this place earlier. I'm going to freshen up and use this restroom one more time," says Wendy.

"Me too! But I want to say this, Twinkie you did a good job. God used you mightily. I wanted to say something but God wouldn't let me. I could only pray. And that's okay. I'm glad I obeyed God. What did Paul say in the Bible?

'I have planted, Apollos watered; but God gave the increase' (1 Corinthians 3:6 KJV).

"We experienced planting in action today. Someone else will water. And God will increase. She will come to God. Let's keep in touch!" says Rosita.

Just then two women come into the restroom. The three women finish freshening up their makeup, use the facilities and wash their hands. They review their hair and faces one last time. They exit the restroom.

Chapter 11
The Truth

Florence sits at the table waiting for Walter to return with the guys. Good! I made it here before he did. I'm also glad that Brandon and Roberta aren't here, Florence thinks. What's with all this new information about Walter being dangerous? My Walter Harris???

I'm not sure what to believe or what not to believe. Walter is so nice and kind to me. He takes care of me. Walter pays for everything. It's hard to find a man that will pay for everything and stay with you. Sure we've had a few bumps along the road but what couple doesn't encounter a snag here or there. Relationships are all about adjusting to one another. Florence thinks.

Sitting there with a glazed look on her face, Florence doesn't even notice the men when they return to the table with Jerred. Walter slips in the seat next to Florence, places his drink in front of him, puts her drink in front of her, and leans towards her ear. Florence jumps and turns around to face Walter.

"Oh Florence, I didn't mean to scare you. I just was going to say, you must be thinking about me with such a deep look on your face. Where are the other ladies?" asks Walter.

"Exactly, what happened to Wendy and Rosita?" asks Percy.

"Oh, I left them in the restroom talking. I wanted to get back to my man, Walter since he just met you guys and he came with me," says Florence.

I don't want to mention that Twinkie was in the restroom with us. I'll just keep that little secret to myself, Florence thinks.

"See gentlemen this is why I love me some Florence. This is exactly why we're engaged! Florence is always thinking about me," says Walter. Percy, Walter, Jerred and Florence talk while waiting for Rosita and Wendy to return. They are joined by Roberta and Brandon, who come back from the dance floor.

In the meanwhile, the three women: Rosita, Wendy and Twinkie head toward the ballroom talking about old times in high school. Right before they enter, Twinkie's husband approaches them.

"Here comes my handsome husband!" says Twinkie.

Now that the contest is over he looks a little familiar to me, thinks Rosita. After he gets closer, Wendy thinks I've seen this man or someone, who looks just like him somewhere. Hershey walks over and kisses Twinkie on her cheek.

"Is everything okay Babe?" asks Hershey.

"Sure is Sugar. Ladies I'd like to introduce you to my husband, Hershey! He's the sweetest and kindest man I know," says Twinkie. Wrapping her arm around Hershey's waist, she introduces them to each other. Starting with Wendy, Twinkie says:

"Sugar this is..."

"Wendy Whitlow! I thought that was you! It's been a long time since I've seen you. That blonde hair is a nice touch," says Hershey as he shakes Wendy's hand. Twinkie is shocked that her husband knows her classmate.

"Wendy Whitlow is correct. But how do you know my name?" asks Wendy. Before Hershey answers Wendy's question, he turns to shake Rosita's hand.

"And if she's Wendy then you must be the missing Julie

Perez! They always said if you find Wendy, she knows what happened to Julie Perez," says Hershey.

Rosita stunned that anyone here other than Wendy and Percy know her real name nods her head indicating "yes." Twinkie looks from one person to another and says,

"No Sugar her name is Rosita not Julie."

"Yes Twinkie, he's right. My name, my birth name is Julie Perez. We changed my name to Rosita Lee right before I came to Preston High School. It's a long story and we did it for safety reasons for both Mama and me. Even with all that, how do you know me because I don't remember you?" says Rosita.

"Look at me closely. Don't I remind you of someone?" asks Hershey. Rosita steps back a little to make sure she sees Hershey for who he is. Rosita looks at Wendy and shrugs her shoulders. Rosita finally asks God under her breath: "who is this man?" Rosita doesn't hear anything from God right away.

Wendy closes one eye and thinks for a minute. Opening her eye up again, Wendy says,

"Well yes, you do remind me of someone but I can't place the face."

"Girl I know! He reminds me of someone too," says Rosita to Wendy. Rosita faces Hershey directly.

"And for you to know both of our last names is unusual. My daddy didn't hire you to find me did he?" asks Rosita.

"No, I lived in Mount Olive, IL. I went to grammar school, middle school and high school there," says Hershey.

"We both lived in Mount Olive, IL. But I don't remember you in any of our classes," says Wendy.

"No I wasn't in your classes. In fact, no one in my family was in any of your classes. You remember the two boys, who used to chase each other and argue at the bus stop every morning?" asks Hershey.

"Oh my God, yes I remember Jerry and Peter. It can't be?" says Wendy with a shocked look in her eyes. Rosita hears right then from God, "Peter's older brother." Rosita and Wendy say it in unison,

"You're Peter's older brother!" Looking at each other, they all laugh.

"I don't remember your name," says Rosita.

"Hershey! Right???" asks Wendy. Hershey nods his head. Wendy hugs Hershey and steps back.

"You look just like him. When did you move here? How is Peter doing? What is he up to?" asks Wendy.

"Wow, Wendy I haven't seen you since you were in grammar school. Remember you graduated from grammar school in the morning. I graduated from high school in the evening the same day. I left for college that summer. You're still the same old Wendy full of questions," says Hershey with a chuckle.

"But before I answer your questions young lady, I want a hug from this here young lady that I haven't seen since your guys were in seventh grade," says Hershey. Rosita/Julie gives Hershey a hug.

"At least, we got a warning about you leaving Mount Olive, Wendy in high school because of your dad and all his medical issues. That was really scary. I'm glad things worked out for him and your family.

"But you: Julie... you just up and disappeared from all of us in Mount Olive. We didn't know what happened to you. One day you were in class and the next day you were nowhere to be found. And it was right around the time Nicole was killed. At first, we all thought you were dead too!"

says Hershey.

"Pete was heartbroken because secretly he had a crush on you, Julie. That's one of the reasons him and Jerry got into it so much. Jerry knew Pete was sweet on you and teased Pete about it all the time. After you left though, Pete sulked all the time. He finally got over it. Then Mom and Dad had to put a restraining order out against your dad," says Hershey. Rosita/Julie nods in understanding.

"Yeah, Mum and Father had to put a restraining order out on Mr. Perez to keep him from me too," says Wendy.

Twinkie stands there in utter amazement! So many thoughts are racing through my mind. Here I am introducing my husband to people he knew when he was younger living in Mount Olive, IL. God: this is a small world, thinks Twinkie.

And now to find out that Rosita Lee had a secret when we were in high school that I never knew about is something else. Wow, her birth name is Julie Perez!!! This has been a real interesting night! A high school reunion filled with different secrets shared by friends, thinks Twinkie.

First my dangerous ex-fiancé Walter Harris is engaged to Florence. And Walter has not changed. Next to find out my husband knew two of my classmates from my high school from when he lived in Mount Olive, IL. Now to find out one of them had a secret before she came to Chicago to Preston High School! If Rosita was already gone, why would Hershey's mom and dad put a restraining order out on Rosita or Julie's dad as Hershey calls her? And Wendy says her parents had a restraining order against Rosita's dad too. What other secrets am I going to find out tonight? I better keep up with what they're saying in case there are more secrets to be revealed, thinks Twinkie.

Hershey looks at his wife for the first time since he realized he is talking with the missing "Julie Perez." Twinkie has a totally dazed look on her face. That's my Babe thinking and listening intently so she knows how to pray. I better let her in on the secret of Julie, thinks Hershey. Before Hershey can talk, Rosita speaks.

I guess I can share my secret with Twinkie, who shared her own personal dangerous secret just a few minutes ago. Rosita thinks.

"Wendy and I knew each other since we were 3 years old. Daddy used to beat Mama. The last time was so bad that one of Mama's eyes was almost completely closed when I went to school the next morning. Blood was everywhere: Mama's blood! The furniture was thrown all over and lamps were shattered. We were in seventh grade at the time. It happened the same night of Nicole's parents' domestic situation.

"Nicole, a girl in our class and her mother, died that next morning from her father beating her mother and accidently hitting Nicole into a wall. That was a wakeup call to my classmates and me about domestic abuse. When we heard about Nicole, I finally told Wendy my secret. It was so embarrassing. But I needed to talk about it with someone I knew I could trust with our family secret. Wendy never told anyone," says Rosita/Julie.

"Mama and I left Daddy that very day. When I came out to the car that afternoon after school, Mama was already packed with all my things including my favorite stuffed animal and blanket. I didn't find out that Mama didn't know about Nicole and her mother until two years later when I told Mama. She never saw the news that night and we were out of town for the funerals. I didn't see

Wendy again until sophomore year of high school, which was three years later.

"Everyone had restraining orders out against Daddy because he started harassing all my classmates and especially those, who caught the bus to school with me. While I was glad Daddy no longer hit Mama, I changed schools and graduated with kids I didn't know. It was hard for me, very hard. Daddy looked everywhere for us. Mama's lawyer convinced the judge to only let Daddy and I visit if it was supervised by my uncle: Big Dee and my abuela, which is grandmother in Spanish," says Rosita/ Julie.

"I'm not the only one, who has been through something like that. I'm glad Mama is still alive. Other people's moms have died. Some people's moms are in jail because they fought back and killed that man in their life. What happened to Mama was so traumatic for me that I majored in counseling in school and at church. My master's degree is in Social Work. I'm certified to counsel. I focus on teenagers and people coping with domestic situations," says Rosita.

Wendy puts her arm around Rosita's shoulder and rubs Rosita's arm for a minute. Wendy asks,

"You okay? You don't sound good."

"I'm okay. I just don't like talking about and revealing my family secret. Now somebody here besides you and Percy know my other name. I'm not sure I'm comfortable with that in this setting. I don't desire to explain to everyone else. It still brings up painful memories.

"I explained it to them because I understand from reading the scriptures and all those lessons at church that husbands and wives shouldn't keep secrets from each other. This is a secret I don't desire Hershey and Twinkie to sweat over or cause an argument between the two of them," says Rosita.

Twinkie shakes her head for a minute then reaches toward Rosita. Pulling Hershey with her they hug Rosita together. Twinkie says,

"No tears now, Rosita. Besides, I know you don't want to make another trip to the restroom to freshen up your makeup now do you?"

All four of them laugh. Placing her arm around Hershey's waist, Twinkie says,

"We won't share your secret with anyone else. We're still friends. My friends are Hershey's friends. I trust him. I remember you keeping my embarrassing secret in high school. No need to worry now. Your secret is safe with us."

Rosita frowns for a moment trying to remember what Twinkie is talking about? Once she recollects, Rosita nods her head and says,

"I was trying to think about, what secret you had? Oh I remember now what you're talking about. Wow, I forgot about that. Thanks."

"In the meantime, Wendy and I had better get back to our table before everything is over. She just got engaged. She has a fiancé to make wedding arrangements with," says Rosita.

"And I think Jerred said something about getting to know Rosita a little better now that she's an adult. I believe Jerred is a little sweet on Rosita," says Wendy smiling.

"You mean that tall light skinned dude she danced with?" asks Hershey.

"Yeah, that be Jerred all right," says Wendy.

"Jerred sweet on me? I don't think so," says Rosita shaking her head to indicate "no."

"That's why I asked, which dude to make sure. When

the guys left the bar with drinks for you ladies, Jerred was looking around and asking people if they knew if Rosita ever came back from the restroom? I think Wendy's right. Jerred is a little sweet on you," says Hershey.

"Before you guys go in, I'm going to ask if we can get together another time. Pete is doing great and maybe I'll invite Pete and Brenise out with us. If you don't know, they got married about two years ago. They have a little girl named Nicole. We have a niece. This way you can keep up with Twinkie and get reacquainted with Pete and Brenise," says Hershey.

"I'm glad you finally answered my questions. Pete and Brenise got married and have a daughter! Wow, I would like to see them. It sounds like a plan to me," says Wendy.

"I'd like that too," says Rosita.

Turning towards Hershey, Twinkie says,

"Sugar, we girls already exchanged business cards. Maybe we can set a date sometime next month. I'll check with Brenise to see what her and Pete's schedule looks like and get back to you in a week if that's okay with you guys?" They all nod in agreement.

"One final thing, I don't think it's good for all of us to go inside together. I don't desire to be the one that Walter recognizes with you guys. If it's okay with you, Hershey and I are going to head towards the bar over there for a few minutes and let you guys enter in alone," says Twinkie.

"It's okay with me," says Rosita.

"Ditto for me," says Wendy.

The four hug each other and part two separate ways. Hershey and Twinkie walk towards the bar while Wendy and Rosita reenter the ballroom. Wendy and Rosita make small talk walking back to the table where they find Percy, Walter, Florence, Jerred, Brandon and Roberta sitting at the table. They pass Jeremiah and Camellita on the dance floor.

"Well it's about time you two returned. You've missed a great discussion," says Percy.

"Yeah, I thought we were going to have to send Ms. Davis to break up your conversation," says Brandon.

"Oh yeah, Man I remember that day under the tree! Or pull the fire alarm to get you girls' attention. Remember Mr. Williams was just getting ready to get the two of you for talking too much in class when the fire alarm went off. We all left the lab, filed outside and walked across the street. Someone pulled the alarm because of the smoke coming from the honors chemistry lab. The fire department came and everything," says Jerred.

"When we started going back in the school, they stayed across the street sitting by that tree just a talking. Ms. Davis, the English teacher only went to get them from under the tree because Rosita and Wendy were too engrossed in their own conversation. Here they are doing it again just like old times. Some people never change," says Jerred.

Everyone started laughing including Rosita and Wendy. Jeremiah and Camellita return to the table. Brandon and Roberta go to the dance floor again.

I'm trying to focus on this conversation but I can't. I have to go to the restroom. But there are still too many men sitting here with Florence at the table. I need them to hurry up and leave, thinks Walter.

Rosita looks around, to see if there are other high school alumni she knows. There must be a way for us to see people we know at the other tables without having to go table to table. Focusing on the table across the room, I can't believe what I'm seeing right now. That must be. That looks like Elizabeth and Preston over there. Rosita thinks.

"Oh my goodness is that Preston and Elizabeth over at that table?" asks Rosita of Wendy in a whisper.

"I think it is," says Wendy in a whisper back.

"I've got to go say something to them. I believe that's Francine with them too. I haven't seen them since graduation," whispers Rosita.

"Neither have I," whispers Wendy.

"Percy! Jerred! Look that's Preston, Elizabeth and Francine at that table over there. Remember them from honors biology sophomore year? I'm going over there with them. This may be the last time I see them," says Rosita.

"I'm coming too," says Wendy as she pushes back her chair.

"You're not leaving me behind this time, Ms. Wendy," says Percy pushing back from the table.

"I can't let you guys go without me. I haven't seen them either. We must go talk with them. Excuse us, we'll be back," says Jerred pushing his chair back from the table.

The four of them: Wendy, Percy, Jerred and Rosita get up to go to the table across the room to talk with Preston, Elizabeth and Francine from honors biology class. The song "Let's Get it On" begins to play. Two couples at the table automatically bob their heads in unison to the rhythm of the music. Although Roberta and Brandon just returned and sat down, they rise with Jeremiah and Camellita. They all ascend to the dance floor again leaving Walter and Florence alone at the table.

Yes, I can go to the restroom now. There are no more

men at the table with Florence, Walter thinks. Turning to Florence, Walter says,

"Baby, I'll be back. I'm going to the restroom." Walter gets up and walks very rapidly toward the restroom.

While heading toward the table with the group, Percy feels uncomfortable. Receiving a check from God, Percy says,

"Guys you go ahead. I'll be along in a few minutes." Under his breath, Percy says, "Yes, Lord. I see Walter leaving. Now is the time for me to talk with Florence."

"Holy Spirit please you give me the right words to say in Jesus name amen," says Percy softly under his breath. "Finally, I get to talk with Florence alone. God is good!" thinks Percy.

Walter is in such a hurry not to have an embarrassing accident in his clothing that he does not look back to see Percy turning around and heading towards the table where Florence is. Florence breathes a cleansing breath as she thinks about what Twinkie said to her. Florence is so deep in thought that she doesn't even notice Percy coming back towards the table.

As Walter heads towards the restroom, he gets direct eye contact with Twinkie sitting next to her husband, Hershey. Hershey does not see Walter's actions. Walter mouths a kiss towards Twinkie. Twinkie grabs Hershey's face, turns it toward her and kisses him. Hershey smiles and kisses Twinkie a second time. Witnessing this angers Walter, who walks even faster to the restroom.

Twinkie saw me! Twinkie knows how good I was to her and she has the nerve to kiss that man in front of me!!! I've got me someone, who I'll never let go of: Florence. My Florence would never disrespect me like that. Florence had better not, thinks Walter.

Percy asks God under his breath to give him enough time to talk with Florence without Walter knowing. God answers Percy's prayer right away. Once Walter gets to the restroom he realizes this is a longer visit here. Walter heads to a stall not the urinal and closes the stall door to sit down.

Percy sits down next to Florence.

"Florence, girl I haven't had a good chance to talk with you alone. You remember our times talking alone after honors English class our junior year?" asks Percy. Florence smiles and says,

"Yes I do. We walked talking about our dreams of what we would do once we graduated from high school. We talked about going to college. As a matter of fact, those conversations inspired me to go to college. I had never thought about it until I talked it over with you. For me, I told you I was going to be the first one in my family to graduate college.

"You said you were going because both your parents were college graduates and to honor your uncle Quentin, who was killed on the corner of 79th and Rhodes. Your uncle Quentin, who was home from college, went to the store for his mom that night. He had one more semester to finish before he graduated with high honors. Your uncle Quentin, who you grew up with and was much younger than your mom, was going to be the second one on your mom's side of the family to graduate college," says Florence.

"You visited your uncle Quentin on campus several times when we were in high school. Your uncle Quentin inspired you to attend college because both he and you were so smart. The two of you were going into business together after you completed college. That dream was shattered when he was killed by that gang member trying to prove his allegiance to his gang.

"What really cinched it for me attending college was your determination to still go to college during the trial and everything else. It propelled me to find the right college, complete the application and attend college even though it was three hours away from home. My parents were so thrilled when I graduated. I never said it but I'm saying it now: thank you!" says Florence.

"You also warned me which guys were trying to play games with my emotions. You warned me of the tricks that were planned for the fat girls to con them. Talking about friends sharing secrets, you were my friend, who shared valuable secrets with me. I never told anyone else.

"Those were the secrets I needed to know so I wouldn't end up like Shaquana, who had a baby by Effrem. Effrem only had sex with Shaquana to prove to the guys he wasn't gay or scared of having sex with a fat girl. Shaquana didn't go to college. As a matter of fact in order for her to finish high school, she transferred to that high school for pregnant teenagers. Even though I attended Shaquana's baby shower, I saw how it damaged her self-esteem. Some people came only to pity her not to be a real friend to her," says Florence.

"I'm also glad you took me to our junior prom even though you wanted to take Wendy and was too scared to ask her. I had a crush on you and you had a crush on Wendy. I remembered at our junior prom: we laughed, made fun of our classmates and danced all night. I had fun and nobody made fun of me being fat. I looked beautiful that night.

"Although we went to the prom as friends, it boosted my self-esteem. I saw myself differently from that point forward. You, Percy were always there for me. I miss our friendship. Thank you for being my friend then," says Florence with tears in the corners of her eyes.

Florence reaches over and gives Percy a hug. Percy receives the hug and embraces Florence back in sincerity. Realizing what she's doing, Florence pulls away from Percy. Quickly, she looks to see if Walter is coming. "Oh my God, Walter can't see me hugging another man. That would cause a problem," thinks Florence. Florence relaxes when she sees Walter still isn't around.

Percy whispers "thank you" to God as he settles back into his seat. Only you God could prepare this platform for me, Percy thinks. Percy puts two fingers to his eyes to pull away tears forming in the corners of his eyes. Trying to be inconspicuous, Percy wipes those tears on his pants leg. I'm a man and men don't cry in front of women, thinks Percy.

"Wow, you remember my uncle Quentin? I forgot you were there as a friend for me. That's right! I remember now. Rosita, Wendy, Jerred, Preston and you came to the wake and the funeral. You were the only one there for me at the repass. That was a hard time for my family and me. You were a great friend too. You were the one, who told me how to go after Wendy. I took you to the prom as my friend but by the end of the night I had a crush on you too! I was totally confused. I was in love with Wendy and really liking you.

"I thought about you all that summer. I was ready to work on being with you that fall but something happened.

You won that writing scholarship to that college in Baltimore where you met a new love. You remember Tony? He was a freshman in college from North Carolina and wealthy. You were just a senior in high school," says Percy. Florence laughs.

"I remember Tony. I was in love with him. Tony took me to our senior prom. His parents came with him to Chicago. They rented a limousine for us; took pictures of us and everything. His parents met my parents for the first time that night and they stayed at the hotel close to our house.

"Tony and I broke up by the end of my freshman year of college. You were the one, who warned me at our senior prom about Tony not being right for me. I didn't believe you because I thought you were jealous of how good Tony was to me. Tony sent me flowers throughout high school and small gifts. You were right about Tony. I should've listened to you. It would've saved me some time," says Florence.

"I remember talking to you after I broke up with him. You listened to me on the telephone mumble, blubber, and cry most of that night. You let me get it all out. You told me I was beautiful even though you hadn't seen me since high school graduation. We only talked back and forth on the phone. I heard you when you said God has someone better for me. And God did!"

"I met Alfred about two months later. Alfred and I dated for the next two years. Alfred was better to me than Tony. We eventually grew apart. But I'm glad I spoke with you that time because when I met Alfred, I was over Tony and ready for a new person in my life," says Florence.

"Thank you Percy for being a friend to me. If you ever have anything to warn me about again, I promise you: I'll listen. I mean it! I know you are a real friend. And I know you won't lie to me," says Florence.

Percy's eyes widen in amazement. God has completely set the stage. This truly is an open door to talk with my old friend about her boo: Walter, Percy thinks. Looking up to see if Walter is coming, Percy talks quickly with Florence.

"Wow, I have a lot to say to you and in a short time. I'm going to start right there. I came back to talk with you alone because God wants you to know that Walter isn't the right one for you now. Walter's not ready to get married to anyone at this moment. This warning about Walter comes directly from God. This isn't the time to get married to Walter.

"God has someone better for you that you'll marry and grow old with together. Someone, who will love you likes Christ loves the church. If it's Walter, then he will get right with God and change completely," says Percy.

"It's God reminding you and me of our friendship in the past. I would like to restart a friendship with you even though I'm engaged to Wendy finally. I desire to give you my phone number. But I've seen guys like Walter react negatively to an innocent friendship and turn it into something ugly in their minds. Give me your number or I'll contact you through Wendy so we can talk more about it, if that's okay with you?" asks Percy.

Looking towards the direction of the restroom, Percy watches to see if Walter is coming back to the table. I don't want Walter to see me talking with Florence. It may not go well for Florence if he does. I'll wait for Florence to respond. It's up to her now, thinks Percy.

Florence looks towards the direction of the restroom. I don't want Walter to see me talking with Percy. First, the girls talking to me about Walter and now Percy! This must be a warning from God for real! I appreciate Percy talking with me but now I've got to find a way to breakup with Walter. How am I going to do that? Florence thinks.

I'm not comfortable giving my number to Percy right now. I remember that family reunion Walter and I attended. Walter got upset because he thought I gave some man my number. (Shuddering slightly, Florence shakes it off.) No I'll go through Wendy to talk with Percy. Where is Walter? How much time do I have to finish this conversation with Percy? Florence thinks.

"I knew I shouldn't have eaten that slice of cheese cake and drank that vodka and orange juice. That cheese cake tasted so good. Uncle Houston always told me not to mix sweets and alcohol. I need to get off this toilet and check on Florence. She'd better not be disrespecting me and talking to some man. Oh my stomach," thinks Walter as he rubs his belly.

"I do want to start our friendship a fresh now that we're both out of college. I believe you're telling me the truth about Walter because you are the second person to talk to me about him tonight. Twinkie talked with me about him in the restroom. Wow! God knows how to get a message to you.

"I don't know how much time I have before Walter gets back? I don't want to give you my number as Walter will ask me, who I gave my number to? I have Wendy's number. We can keep contact through her if that's okay with you? I'm also scared for Walter to see me talking with you. Thank you!" says Florence. Looking toward the restroom direction one more time, Florence smiles as Percy rises.

"Florence: remember God has someone better for you.

Wendy and I will be praying for you," says Percy. Percy walks away. Percy joins Rosita, Jerred and Wendy at the other table across the room.

Wrapping his arm around Wendy's shoulder, Percy leans in and whispers in Wendy ear,

"Please agree with me that Father God helps Florence. That God protects her and Florence receives Jesus in her heart right now in Jesus name amen."

Wendy whispers back, "I agree in Jesus name amen." Percy then kisses Wendy softly on her cheek. Wendy smiles and kisses Percy on his cheek.

"You guys remember that time Francine and Elizabeth destroyed their project in honors biology by pouring acid on the specimen instead of water to lessen the smell?" asks Rosita as she winks to Percy.

The whole group laughs including Percy, who joined the conversation.

"Thank you God for using me tonight," whispers Percy under his breath. Percy, Wendy, Jerred, Rosita, Francine, Elizabeth and Preston continue reminiscing about honors biology.

Florence sips her drink and places her glass on the table. Florence hears those words she heard so many times before from her teetee Yolanda about how to receive Jesus in her heart. Florence prays.

"God I know that this warning is from you. Please don't let any man be at this table when Walter returns. God help me to know you right now. My teetee Yolanda says if I call on Jesus, he'll help me. Well tonight Jesus: I'm calling on you. I need you to help me. Jesus, I need to know you for myself.

Twinkie was right: I don't know you. Jesus I'm sorry for my sins. I repent. Please forgive me. Come into my heart. Be my Lord and savior. I need you, Jesus in my heart for real right now," says Florence.

Suddenly Florence feels a peace come over her heart and body. Florence looks up. Walter is walking toward her direction. Good nobody is at this table, Florence thinks. As Walter walks toward Florence, he meets Roberta and Brandon coming off the dance floor. Talking with them, Walter slows his pace returning to the table. "Good no man is sitting with Florence," thinks Walter. Florence continues praying.

"I need you Jesus to protect me from Walter. I don't want him to hit me. Jesus: please help me break up with Walter. Show me how, when and where to do it, in Jesus' name amen." says Florence.

Brandon, Roberta and Walter return to the table. The rest of the night goes smoothly. Slowly one-by-one individuals and couples leave to prepare for the picnic on the following day. Wendy rides to the apartment with Percy so they can talk alone. Jerred makes plans to pick up Rosita for the picnic so she can ride there with him. As Rosita drives to the apartment and reminisces about the evening, she thanks God for using her tonight and for all the good reconnections of friendships. Rosita says to God,

"Thank you Jesus for being in my life. Thank you for loving me. I thank you for protecting Florence. I thank you for Wendy finally getting with Percy. And they're engaged! He's the one for her. I thank you Jesus for all the good friendships and reconnections. I thank you for Jerred and me talking again. I appreciate you in my life so much. I'm so grateful I can talk to you anytime. I ask that we have a great time at the picnic tomorrow in Jesus name amen!"

Rosita parks her car. Looking up to their apartment, there are no lights on in the apartment yet. Oh well, I'll get details from Wendy about her engagement another time. Our conversation can wait because Wendy is not getting married tomorrow. Knowing Wendy, she's probably somewhere talking nonstop.

Wow! I'm glad we did not get that condo like we started to! What are we going to do about this apartment if they decide to get married right away? "Although she's not married yet, we have time to figure everything out," says Rosita to herself out loud.

Oh my! If things get serious with Jerred and me, I'll have to tell him my other name. I'm really sleepy. I'll cross that bridge when I come to it. I'm going to bed, Rosita thinks. After hanging up her dress, changing into her pajamas; wrapping up her hair and turning out the light; Rosita crawls into her bed. Rosita smiles as she closes her eyes. Tonight was exciting, a good workout and a blessing, thinks Rosita.

Four

Months

Later

Chapter 12
Dreams Come True

Wendy is not home from work yet. Julie prepares for her date with Jerred. She looks through her closet for something blue to wear. Julie pulls out her blue, red and white dress. Holding it up, I think I can wear this. It is a mixture of both Jerred's favorite color and my favorite color with purity white added. I look okay in this, thinks Julie.

Hum, I seem to remember I have a solid electric blue dress. I'll put this blue, red and white dress back. Where is it? Pushing some clothes along the closet rod, here it is: my electric blue dress! I think I'll wear this dress tonight instead. Between the two dresses, I look best in this! Julie pulls it out of her closet and hangs it on the hook outside her closet door.

Jerred is getting used to calling me Julie instead of Rosita. I like that. Jesus you know that Jerred is something else. Jerred shared with me that he used to tease me so much in high school because he liked me. I thought back then Jerred was just joking to get laughs from others. Jerred also shared that he always wanted to go on a date with me but couldn't find the right time or the words to ask me nor ever had enough money to do it, thinks Julie.

As a matter of fact, Jerred said he dreamed about dating me right after we graduated high school. He didn't know how to find me to make that dream come true. Jerred finally got the nerve to search for me at my college my sophomore year. But he didn't know I had changed back to my birth name.

Jerred was so glad I made it to the reunion because now he envisioned the possibility of his dreams manifesting.

He thanked you Jesus for making his dreams come true. Jerred said "dreams" because the closer he got to you, the more he had dreams of being my friend and dating me. Dreams I would be his special friend or best friend and his girl. We have become best friends so quickly. Wow! Look at us today. You: Jesus made it happen. You are fulfilling Jerred's dreams, thinks Julie.

Stepping back, Julie closes her eyes for a moment. She tries to envision which shoes to wear that won't hurt her feet and will look great with the dress. Opening her eyes, Julie says out loud, "I think I'll wear those black patent leather pumps I got from that designer store. They'll set this dress off just right. I'll look fabulous again tonight!"

Moving shoes around on the floor she locates the shoes, pulls them out of the closet and places them on the floor next to the chair in her room she uses for dressing.

Looking at her watch and setting it, Julie walks to her bed. "I have an hour and a half to rest before I really have to get dressed," thinks Julie.

Lying on her bed, Julie allows her thoughts to overtake her mind. So many different things have transpired since my 10th year high school class reunion dinner. Who knew God could work situations and issues out so quickly? Who knew God would use my high school reunion to answer so many questions and prayers? And who knew so many people were still or could still be friends sharing each other's secrets?

The picnic the following day after our 10th year high school reunion dinner was nice. It was a good day to have the picnic. The sun was out with a few clouds and the location was great. Less people showed up than had been expected. Some people brought their children. I'm glad I did not have to bring food as it was included in the price of the class reunion, thinks Julie.

I'm also very grateful I wore my red shorts outfit. I looked fabulous as usual. I got to visit with some people, who did not make it to the dinner the night before. While I enjoyed myself, I was very glad when it was all over.

I was so tired I slept hard that night. Although I went to church the next day, I didn't stay like I normally would have. I sat at the back of the church so I could run out of there as fast as I could to get home to my bed. My car was at the end of the parking lot to ease my exit plan. Wendy must have been that tired herself as she beat me home into her bed. I saw her briefly at church. That Sunday was not a fellowship Sunday for me, thinks Julie.

Rehearsing the events in her mind, Julie continues to allow her thoughts to flow. Two days after that, Wendy shared with me her long time secret of how she liked Percy in high school but knew he wasn't a Christian. Wendy told me how she prayed at a church revival for Percy to receive Jesus in his heart when she was in high school. Here it is 12 plus years later. Not only has Percy received Jesus in his heart but Wendy and Percy are engaged to get married! Wow!

Wendy confided to me that when she saw Percy standing there taller than both she and me, Wendy felt woozy like she did in high school all over again. While Wendy was glad I stayed behind at the reception table so she could talk with Percy alone, Wendy wondered if she was being foolish thinking that way about Percy? Earl was sitting with Percy when Wendy got to the table. Wendy sat down. Listening to Percy, she knew something was different about him. At first, Wendy thought it was Percy's deep voice and height, thinks Julie.

Wendy always did like guys, who were tall. So much so that she'd stop walking wherever we were as teenagers, turn her body and follow those guys with her eyes until they got out of her sight. That's probably why she never shared with me her secret crush on Percy. Percy was definitely shorter that both of us in high school.

Now the God details, ponders Julie. As Wendy listened, she realized Percy's whole demeanor had changed and it was not just the fact he was older. So while Percy talked with Earl, who Percy used to run with in high school, Wendy asked God: what is so different about Percy now? God answered Wendy right away. Wendy said she heard God very clearly that night. God reminded Wendy of her prayer all those years earlier. God said He answered Wendy's prayer for Percy to get saved! God told Wendy He preserved Percy for her. God then asked Wendy: do you want Percy as your husband? Wendy immediately said "yes" to God, thinks Julie.

Who wouldn't? I'd said "yes" too! Wendy had been praying for a godly man to come into her life and here God brings that man directly to her door! Moreover it's the guy she had a crush on in high school! Talking about a Cinderella story line come true! Wendy said she used to dream of being married to Percy in high school.

Wendy said she was so scared to share her secret dreams with me about Percy in high school because Percy was not saved. Wendy admitted she also was terrified of talking to her mum about Percy for that same reason. Wendy talked to the only person she could about Percy: Jesus. Wendy said she left her thoughts about Percy on the altar that night in church at that revival where she asked God to save Percy's life when we were in high school. Wendy said she felt a special peace about Percy from that moment forward. Wendy said from time to time whenever God brought thoughts of Percy to her mind Wendy prayed for Percy and felt peaceful, thinks Julie.

"Wow, I get goose bumps when I think about what Wendy said next." Julie says out loud. Going back to her thoughts, Julie ponders some more. Wendy said all of a sudden, she felt God's presence right there in the ballroom! When Earl left the table, Wendy felt that same peace surrounding her from God that she felt that night at the church's revival. Wendy was so calm that when Percy looked at her and started talking again, she was very relaxed. Percy said,

"I'm glad Rosita is not here so I can talk to you one-on-one. I forgot how peaceful I always felt around you in high school and I'm feeling that same peace right now. Wendy it took me years to get to this point. I have something to say to you. I know how you like to talk but please allow me to finish before you say anything." Wendy said she couldn't speak anyway. She was too astonished. So Wendy said she just nodded her head, thinks Julie.

Percy continued. "I knew from the first time I saw you in your brown outfit with that white sweater in high school, I loved you. We were only teenagers and I found out that you believed in Jesus. My aunts talked about Jesus before and how they were waiting for Jesus to bring their men to them. While I didn't want to hear that about you, I was very intrigued. I watched how you wouldn't compromise your standards. While I made fun of you and your Jesus, I was very jealous of your relationship with him. I wondered: how could you or anyone be so in love with Jesus and still be in a natural relationship?"

Percy said to Wendy.

"About four years ago, I received Jesus in my heart. It was a turning point in my life. I worshipped and appreciated Him for saving me in the midst of all my ugly mess. Jesus loved me at the cross and still loves me today. King Jesus introduced me to Holy Spirit. In prayer a little later, I asked Holy Spirit: who am I going to marry? I waited to hear from God. In a dream, I saw you, Wendy like I did that first time in high school in honors biology class dressed in brown pants and brown boots with a white sweater. The scene changed. I saw you when we graduated from high school and you wore all purple under our red robes. The last part of my dream I'll tell you about in a few minutes," thinks Julie.

Percy next said to Wendy: "when I woke up, God told me I would see you again. I didn't R.S.V.P. for this reunion until I heard you were coming. Now that I see you, you are more beautiful than when I first met you. On the way over here God said I could ask you two questions. Question number one: are you in a relationship with another physical man?" Percy asked.

Wendy, who could not talk before that moment, whispered "No."

Percy smiled. Looking up Percy said out loud,

"Lord you are amazing!" Getting down on one knee, Percy pulled a ring out from his pocket. He reached for Wendy's right hand and asked,

"Wendy Whitlow will you marry me?"

Wendy said she looked directly into Percy's eyes. While she was very excited, she felt so much peace flood her heart. Smiling, Wendy said "yes." Percy slipped a ring on her finger. It was too big and very loose. Wendy said she did not care about that because that could be fixed. What Wendy did care about was: God had brought her man of God to her. God answered her prayers! And God gave her the option of accepting her man of God, thinks Julie.

After Wendy said "yes," Percy got up and kissed Wendy full on her lips. Next Percy said,

"This was the last part of my dream. Me proposing to you on my one knee and you saying yes! Thank you for fulfilling my dream." Right after that Percy sat down. Percy was looking into Wendy's eyes, when I arrived at the table.

Now Percy and Wendy are making wedding plans to get married next year. Wendy is so excited! She has been studying the Bible even more than before. Wendy realized Percy and her dating as an engaged couple is just like it was in biblical days for Mary and Joseph. Percy declared his honorable intentions right up front. Thus, there is no mistake! He desires to marry her. She is dating her mate, her intended! Julie thinks.

Wow! I remember Wendy sharing that secret with me. She desired to know a man's honorable intentions up front, which is why Wendy rarely dated anyone before. Her mum was always trying to set Wendy up with those church guys, who had no real desire to marry Wendy. The three men, who finally agreed to go out with Wendy from her mum's arrangements only wanted to get in the bed with her with no commitment. And they were from various churches!

Where was their honorable commitment to God? Never mind the fact that Wendy is a virgin like myself saving herself for her husband, which is her honorable commitment to God. Her mum wanted grandchildren and Wendy was taking too long to hook up with someone. Wendy shared how she constantly felt the pressure from her mum to find somebody as soon as possible, thinks Julie.

When I picked her up from her date at the restaurant in Oak Brook, IL that last time, it solidified her decision. Wendy called me from the restroom. Her date had put his hand on her thigh. It was their first date! Wendy was appalled! He apologized when Wendy popped his hand. He said he did it because she was so beautiful that he couldn't help himself.

One of his female friends showed up at their table while they were eating. When her date started explaining himself to his female friend for being there with Wendy, Wendy sent me a text, asking me how far away was I? It was good I was shopping at the Oak Brook Mall that night. I had just finished purchasing my items from her previous phone call and was at that restaurant within a few minutes, thinks Julie.

Wendy's date was so engrossed in his female friend and himself that when she excused herself to go to the restroom a second time, he did not notice Wendy grabbed her coat also. She was so angry. She vented all the way home. We prayed that night after we got home and she calmed down. Wendy forgave that man then asked God for a man, who would love her as Christ loves the church. She asked for a man, who would declare and show his honorable intentions up front. There would be no questions at all. Wendy asked God that He pick out the man for her not her mum. Wendy asked God that her mum stop acting like she was still a little girl and treat her like a woman able to make her own choices.

Wendy also asked God to keep her mum busy with other things so Wendy would no longer feel the pressure to get married because her mum got married at 19 and Wendy was now older than that. Wow! God you answered our prayer through Percy. Talking about the power of the prayer of agreement, it manifested in full force! Wendy has been a lot more quiet and reserved. I guess you God are constantly speaking and confirming things to her, thinks Julie.

Wendy's colors for their wedding are white, purple and silver. Percy's favorite color is brown but he wants to see Wendy work on her purple color scheme for the wedding. They will use brown, lavender and silver for the wedding rehearsal dinner. She and Percy are now looking for places to hold the wedding reception. Wendy met Percy's parents officially as an adult. She's been to his church several times. Percy met Wendy's mum and Father. Percy asked Wendy's father f it was okay for him to marry his daughter. Wendy's father said "yes" to Percy for Wendy to get married to. Wow! And I'm going to be her maid of honor. Wow! God this is all so awesome!

Next her thoughts go back to the reunion dinner. Yeah, God what about Florence? (Julie thinks about the things that happened with Florence in the order they occurred.)

Florence lost all that weight, over 100 pounds! And she kept it off for over seven years. That is a miracle! Florence looks so amazing! But with all that weight loss externally and looking great, Florence still required an internal overhaul. She hadn't changed in her spirit, thinks Julie.

A week after the reunion, I got a call from Twinkie. I'm so glad she called me. We discussed what happened our reunion night. I thanked her for sharing her secret with Wendy, Florence and me. I revealed I knew Florence was in trouble when I saw her get out of her car and Walter linked his arm into Florence's arm. I shared how Walter made a pass at me that same night. I shared what happened to Mama. I told Twinkie about Kim and Chris' new girlfriend from college.

Twinkie said she did not have an answer from Pete and Brenise for us to get together or set a date. She would get back to me on that, thinks Julie.

Twinkie shared how she'd been praying for Florence and wanted another woman to agree with her in prayer to save Florence's life. After we prayed for Florence, God, you gave me specific instructions. We were to set up a lunch date with Florence within a week and include Wendy. Since Twinkie was the farthest away, we worked on two days the following week. This gave Twinkie time to get here in the Chicago area.

Next, I, not Twinkie was to invite Florence since Twinkie was Walter's old fiancée. This way Florence would only have my telephone number in her cell phone not Twinkie's. We didn't want to raise suspicion or reveal any of God's strategy. God, you said specifically lunch so that Walter would be preoccupied with his job. God, you also said for us to take two or more hours off our jobs even if Florence could only make it for 45 minutes, one hour or an hour and a half. You told us to select a location near her job that was easy access for her. You, God revealed this was war for her life, thinks Julie.

I thanked Twinkie for calling me. I found Florence's number and called her. I told Wendy what we were doing. Her spirit quickly agreed to participate. She wanted in on the ability to obey God and watch Him work. Wow! Wendy shared how God had her and Percy praying for Florence too since our reunion. I desired to know: how come I didn't have the 411 prayer memo about Florence from the reunion night?

When Florence didn't answer within 24 hours, I sent her a text. I also asked you God for further instructions. You said have Wendy contact Florence too. I told Wendy and she did. Florence responded to Wendy first then to me. She checked her schedule and could make it on the following Thursday. There were two restaurants near her job that Florence suggested. We set a time of 1:30 p.m. When I finalized our lunch date, I told her we would see her there. Florence sounded excited to meet with us and said she had exciting news to share with us, thinks Julie.

On Sunday night Twinkie called around 7:30 p.m. She conferenced Wendy and me in on the phone. As we prayed, God you gave more instructions for the next three days. We were to eat no sweets, no chips and no meat. We were to drink no sugar like sodas, no coffee and no tea. We could only eat vegetables and fruits without bread or crackers. Our only liquid was water. God you also said ask the guys if they would join us.

The agreed consecration was to save Florence's life from death, for her to see the truth about Walter, Walter to see the truth about himself; and for both of them to get saved. Hershey and Percy immediately agreed when Wendy and Twinkie spoke with them. They knew what kind of man Walter is, thinks Julie.

I hesitated in calling Jerred. So God you had Jerred call me about half an hour later. Jerred was his comical cheerful self at first until he shared what was really on his heart. I heard the seriousness in his voice. Jerred talked about how he watched Walter and Florence at our reunion. Jerred suggested he and I pray for them because something was seriously wrong. He saw the look on Florence's face when they lost the contest. Since Florence was our old friend, God you prompted Jerred to get Walter away from Florence right at that moment. Jerred did just that! Wow! Jerred hears from you God and acts on it.

At that point, I shared the prayer and consecration strategy given by you God for Florence and Walter. Jerred quickly agreed and asked me: why hadn't I called him to have him included right away? I admitted to Jerred I hesitated because I didn't know how he would react? I've talked with guys about spiritual things before and they thought I was being nosy or too spiritual. One man told me it was none of my business and things were not that deep. These men went to church and were supposed to have a relationship with Jesus, thinks Julie.

I wasn't sure if he, Jerred would understand and not call me weird. I repented and said I should have trusted God. Jerred said he was glad he obeyed God and called right then. Jerred confided in me that he loved spiritual assignments and challenges! Jerred explained that he looked at it this way: when we complete our spiritual assignments or challenges, we grow.

Then Jerred said I could talk with him about anything or ask him to pray about anything. When Jerred said that I knew he had grown spiritually, that Jerred really knows you God and loves you. I believed him. In that moment, I relaxed and knew Jerred was telling me the truth. Wow! A possible male Christian friend like Wendy, thinks Julie.

Tuesday night at about 6 p.m. of that week, I received a call from Florence. She sounded strange. She asked me how much was the pizza? Then she asked how much was delivery? She asked me to explain the difference in prices between deep dish and thin crust. I left my bedroom and walked directly into Wendy's bedroom without even knocking. I put Florence on speaker so Wendy could hear. Wendy pulled out the menu from one of our pizza places and talked about the prices. I heard trembling in Florence's voice, thinks Julie.

"Is he still there?" I asked.

"Yes, I think the thin crust is best," said Florence.

"Should we call the police?" asked Wendy.

"No deep dish may be too thick to chew right now," said Florence. She sighed heavily. We heard noises in the background and a door slam.

"I'll check my purse to see if I have enough money to pay for this delivery. Could you have a woman deliver it please?" asked Florence.

Wendy asked a second time should she call the police?

"No, I believe I'll stick with that thin crust. You can have a woman deliver. Oh good thank you. I understand. The woman will not have the standard pizza car as the other men drivers have all of them. That's okay with me. No I don't think I want to use a credit card tonight," said Florence.

"We'll pray for you right now. Do you want to give us your address so we can deliver it?" I said.

"Okay here's my address. Yes, you can put it in the system for now. I can't locate me purse right now. Please do not put the order through if I don't call you back in 15 minutes. I need to locate my purse so I can pay you in cash. Now that is a medium cheese and green peppers pizza. I know you have a special, which includes a pop but I don't want the pop. Yes this is the right telephone number. Thank you. I'll call in 15 minutes, bye," said Florence. I wrote down Florence's address, thinks Julie.

Wendy started praying in tongues. I called Twinkie and Jerred with Wendy's cell phone in case Florence's phone was confiscated by Walter and he called my number. I apprised them of the situation. Twinkie said she and Hershey would be praying together. Jerred began praying while I was on the telephone. I told him I would share any developments and I got off the telephone. When I finished I gave Wendy her cell phone back. She called Percy to pray too.

I waited and exactly 15 minutes later, Florence called. I placed her call on speaker again. Wendy came into my bedroom. Wendy asked,

"Is he still there?"

Florence said,

"Yes, I found my purse and I have enough money. You still have my order in the system? Yes, you are right the medium thin crust cheese pizza with green peppers. You can put that order through now. Good. Could you add a small salad to it please?"

Wendy said,

"Do you want us to come by and bring this over?"

"Yes, I'd like a salad added if you can," said Florence.

"Yes we can and we'll bring it by your place." I said.

"You can add the salad. Good! What kind of salads do you have?" asked Florence. I changed into my loose jeans, a sweat shirt, and gym shoes. I pulled a hat out of my closet to cover my hair, thinks Julie.

"Oh, your small salads are house salads with only lettuce, tomatoes, and cucumbers. What kind of dressing do you have? You have ranch, Italian, French and the house dressing. Okay, I'll take the house dressing please. How long will that take?" asked Florence.

"We should be able to get there with everything in about an hour to an hour and a half depending on the pizza place and the traffic," said Wendy.

"Oh you're really busy tonight. Okay about an hour or an hour and an a half? That should be fine. Thank you for taking my order and upgrading it. Bye," said Florence, thinks Julie.

After Florence hung up, Wendy sprang into action. She went to her bedroom and changed her clothes into her jeans, a tee shirt and gym shoes. Wendy also called Percy to follow us as backup in case of trouble. I called Jerred. Five minutes later just as I was getting ready to place the pizza order and right before we walked out of the door, Florence called back. I put her on speaker again. She whispered.

"Guys, he left. I'm okay. Did you order the pizza yet? If not, please don't. You don't have to come by. I have an important meeting at work very early tomorrow morning. I just have a black eye and he threw the furniture around. I've got to work on this eye so that it is not so noticeable in the morning. Walter packed a bag, left for a business trip and won't be back until Monday," said Florence. Julie thinks.

I asked her if she was sure she didn't want us to come by?

Florence said,

"No, I heard someone say to me: 'Go to your mother's house tonight.' I didn't go because I had that meeting to prepare for and Mom's house is really noisy. I realized it was God, who said that earlier. I prayed and asked Jesus in my heart that night at our reunion. He was guiding me and I did not recognize His voice. I should have listened.

"I had no idea Walter was going to act like that.

Supposedly, he has an unexpected out-of-town business meeting that he did not know about. I asked him if we could go to church with my teetee Yolanda. Walter got very angry. He started throwing the furniture around. I ran toward the bedroom door. Walter started yelling something about me going to church to meet new men? That's when he grabbed me and hit me several times in my eye. I was screaming so loudly," said Florence, thinks Julie.

"After he hit me, Walter said,

'Well you won't want to go to church now and if you do, no man will want you.' I started crying and trying to get out the front door so I could leave and call somebody. I got the front door opened. Walter grabbed me while the front door was opened. As he raised his hand to strike me again, this time I shouted, '**JESUS! JESUS! J EE S U S!**'" said Florence.

"Walter released me and said, 'Look at what you made me do? You know I love you. I'm sorry. I have to go.' After that Walter got his keys, his wallet, his bag, his cell phone and left. He drove away. It caught me so by surprise since nothing that violent had happened from him towards me in a long time.

"I feel a peace now that Walter is gone. I hear that I can stay because he's not coming back tonight. It's the same voice that told me to go to Mom's house. I should have listened. I thank Jesus that like my mama and my teetee Yolanda say, 'there is power in the name of Jesus,'" said Florence, thinks Julie.

Wendy and I stood in shock looking at each other, realizing at how much Florence had grown spiritually in such a short time. Then we praised you Jesus while Florence was on the telephone that she was alright.

Wendy said,

"If you want us to come by we still can." At that point, I shook my head no because I could clearly hear you God saying not to go. Julie thinks.

"No, I'm hearing right now to call my teetee Yolanda. She'll help me. TeeTee Yolanda has been telling me all along that Walter was not right for me. God is telling me to get in contact with her. After I hang up with you, I'll call her. Are we still on for Thursday?" asked Florence.

I said,

"Yeah, girl, I have some things to share with you. I also want to hear how you gave your life to Jesus! Praise God! Amen!"

"Praise God! Good, I'll see you then. Huh, oh, someone must have called the police," said Florence. Through the phone we heard:

"POLICE: OPEN UP! IS EVERYTHING OKAY IN THERE?"

"The police are banging at the door. I'll text you after they leave to let you know everything is okay. I've got to go. Love you," said Florence.

"JUST A MINUTE HERE I COME!" shouted Florence. We heard furniture moving, thinks Julie.

"Bye" said Florence and hung up her cell phone. I plugged my cell phone in so that it would charge back up.

Wen and I talked about how you God had answered prayer again. Then as we were praising you, Percy and Jerred knocked on our door. They were waiting outside expecting to follow us in one car. When we did not come down, they decided to come up and see if there was a problem. Wendy explained what happened with Florence to Percy and Jerred while I called Twinkie. I moved my cell phone from my bedroom to our living room while it was on the charger. I put Twinkie on speaker as she requested to address us all, thinks Julie.

Twinkie said,

"This is not over. This is only the beginning. We still have to pray. Florence is still in there in danger. God is telling me there is more. That is why she still agreed to meet us for lunch. I have Hershey right here next to me. I'm going to put you on our speaker too. Let us all pray together. Remember our focus is:

1. to save Florence's life from death
2. for her to see the truth about Walter
3. for Walter to see the truth about himself
4. for both of them to get saved not just Florence
5. for both of them to get delivered."

Hershey spoke out loud the foundational scriptures for our prayer of agreement. He said,

- *"The Lord is not slack concerning his promise, as some men count slackness; but is longsuffering to us-ward, not willing that any should perish but that all should come to repentance (2 Peter 3:9 KJV).*

- *But as many as received him, to them gave he power to become the sons of God, even to them that believe on his name (John 1:12 KJV):*

- *Christ hath redeemed us from the curse of the law, being made a curse for us: for it is written, Cursed is every one that hangeth on a tree: That the blessing of Abraham might come on the Gentiles through Jesus Christ; that we might receive the promise of the Spirit through faith (Galatians 3:13-14 KJV).*

- *And Jesus looking upon them saith, With men it is impossible, but not with God: for with God all things are possible" (Mark 10:27 KJV).*

Julie thinks.

At first, we held hands while we prayed. Then slowly one by one we all got on our knees that night. Each one of us took turns praying on the behalf of both Florence and Walter. While we women wanted only to pray for Florence, I was glad the men were there praying for Walter. They really knew what to pray and how to pray.

We bound generational curses, fear, frustration, doubt, low self-esteem, anger, unbelief, hatred, and other things. We loosed your change, protection, deliverance, love, joy, breakthrough and new lives. We prayed as a group until you God gave us the release to stop. Then we praised you God for the changes and for the breakthrough. While praising you God, it happened. We felt a spiritual shift full of your presence and anointing. We all physically experienced it. Wow, that night was awesome and powerful! Julie thinks.

After the guys left, I checked my messages. Florence had texted me to tell me that her teetee Yolanda came. At first, she was not going to press charges. The police are mandatory reporters so they took pictures of her face and the condo. The police team was a woman and a man. When they could not get Florence to come to the precinct to press charges against Walter, the police left. After her teetee Yolanda arrived and talked with Florence, Florence filed charges against Walter. Florence also went to the hospital for a doctor's report. TeeTee Yolanda stayed with Florence that night.

When Thursday came, you God told me to tell my supervisor, I would not be back for that afternoon. I did just that. Unbeknown to me, God you told Wen the same thing. (She told me later.) I took half a day off so that I could meet Wen and drive in with her and Twinkie in one car. That saved on gas and it allowed us to pray together on the way there. We arrived at this large restaurant. We found a booth in the corner on the west side away from everyone so that we could talk freely. I waited up front for Florence to arrive, thinks Julie.

When she did, Florence wore those huge dark sun glasses like Mama wore after Daddy hit her. I saw where her left eye was still a little dark. We hugged and I took her to where Wen and Twinkie were seated. She melted when she saw Twinkie. Tears came to Florence's eyes, she had us all crying. The three of them got their hugs out and everyone sat down. Florence's back was to the door so she could not see the people entering or leaving. We dried our tears then began talking and laughing. We were all having a good time talking about high school, Jesus, Florence's conversion to Him and our secret dreams.

We had finished eating the appetizers and just after the salad arrived, this man entered with a woman to be seated. The man looked a little familiar. The woman he was with wore a plunging neckline on a very short two-piece dress. He rubbed his hand up and down her backside. She was smiling with her arm wrapped around his waist. It was noticeable because her short skirt was moving up and down revealing more than it should. People's heads turned as this couple passed by them. There were no more seats on our side of the restaurant so the hostess seated them on the east side of the restaurant. We were further away so I really could not completely see his face. But that man initially looked familiar to me, thinks Julie.

"This is a very popular restaurant. The food is fresh and fabulous! It's always crowded. I'm glad we did not have to wait. I'm also surprised you were already seated before I got here. They don't usually do that. Wait until you taste your main entrees," said Florence.

"I agree the food is fresh and fabulous. This bread reeks of freshness. The whiff is so tantalizing to my nostrils and I can smell the freshness of this butter too," said Twinkie.

Shaking our heads, we all laughed. Twinkie still had that wonderful descriptive use of words as she did in high school. Right then I had to use the ladies' room. I told them I was headed for the restroom so I could enjoy my food. I invited the others to join me. Only Wendy responded. Twinkie went when we first arrived and Florence went before she left work, thinks Julie.

We walked to the center of the restaurant where the restrooms were. Turning the corner, we could not see but we heard a couple talking from the booth on the other side of the thin partition. The conversation stopped us in our tracks. The couple was talking about a woman named Florence. Was it our Florence? We listened for a minute.

"I bet Florence don't feed you like this in the restaurant," said the woman.

"Naw Baby, Florence don't feed me like this nor wear her clothes like you do," said the man.

"When you gonna leave Florence and come stay with me always instead of just a few times in a month? You know I know how to hit your button. Where Florence think you at anyway?" said the woman.

"You're right Baby. You know how to hit my button. Florence thinks I'm out of town on business. I am out of her eye sight taking care of you," said the man.

"Yes, you are," said the woman.

"You think Florence is with someone else like you're with me?" asked the woman.

"I took care of Florence real good before I left. She ain't with nobody else. Why we got to talk about Florence? I'm here with you. Can we focus on you?" asked the man, thinks Julie.

Wendy and I looked at each other. Scrunching up our noses, we shook our heads and I narrowed my eyes. It couldn't be Walter, could it? The man's voice sounded like Walter's! I whispered to Wendy, I really have to go. Besides, he may recognize me.

Wendy said in a whisper,

"I'm going to see. Who is this man? It could be somebody else."

I went into the restroom and Wendy followed shortly thereafter. After she and I relieved ourselves, we washed our hands. We waited for this other woman to leave the restroom before talking, thinks Julie.

"It is Walter! I'm glad he didn't see me. He might not have seen you anyway. Walter was so busy in that woman's face. Besides, he is sitting right next to her in the booth on the same side with his arm wrapped around the woman's waist while she is feeding him fruit! We can't let Florence see Walter right now. We've gotta keep her at the table." said Wendy. I was glad I had my purse and cell phone with me.

"No! We do not keep her at the table. This may be the final thing that makes Florence realize what kind of man Walter really is. I believe this is a God setup. I'm texting Twinkie so she will go to the restroom with Florence after we get back. Florence will not believe us if we told her. She'll have to hear it and see it for herself," I said, thinks Julie.

I wrote out my text, made sure it was only addressed to Twinkie and sent it. Grabbing a paper towel, I reached for the door, opened it, let Wendy go out first, threw that paper towel in the garbage right by the door and left the restroom. When we got to the table our main entrees were there. Shortly after we started eating our food, Twinkie excused herself to go to the restroom and grabbing her purse, she invited Florence along telling her she didn't want to go alone. Florence reluctantly left her food. She and Twinkie talked along the way to the restroom.

We waited a moment then followed a ways behind them without Florence seeing us. Turning into the hallway Twinkie and Florence continued walking until Florence heard her name. She stopped right in her tracks. Twinkie filled us in later on what was said, thinks Julie.

"Wait a minute, Twinkie are they talking about me?" Florence whispered. Listening to the conversation, Florence eyes got really big. Florence covered her hand over her mouth.

"You know we in public. Since your Florence French thinks you're on a business trip, how come you can't stay longer with me Walter Harris? You can extend your business trip you know," said the woman, thinks Julie.

When the woman called out Walter's name, both Twinkie and Florence released gasps of air. Wendy and I were close by watching the two of them as they listened to the conversation. What was so interesting is Walter and that woman's conversation was loud. Florence was so aghast that she did not see us watching her and trying to listen to them, thinks Julie.

"What you gonna do if I extend my business trip and stay with you until the middle of next week Jenny?" asked Walter.

"I'll..." (Whatever she said was whispered in Walter's ear, because no one heard it.)

"Well... well all right now. But how you gonna get out of work? You know Florence works for you," said Walter.

"I've got vacation time. Besides, I'm the boss. I have some very labor intensive work I can give Florence to keep her busy. If that doesn't work, there are two other meetings in the next two weeks I'll have Florence prepare for. If I give Florence the other meetings to research and prepare for, you got to stay with me until the end of the next week until I'm completely satisfied. That means you don't go home to your Florence until Sunday next week. You gonna be able to stay away from your Florence French that long? Or you think Florence French gonna be with someone else?" asked Jenny, thinks Julie.

"I told you I took care of Florence French real good so that she wouldn't be with no one else while I'm gone. I know how to handle my business. I'm the only one, who gets to play in this thing. Now give me some sugar," said Walter. Jenny and Walter kiss several times. You heard their kisses.

"Stop it. We got to eat to keep our strength up for this afternoon, tonight, tomorrow, this weekend and all next week," said Jenny.

"Okay, I'll stop for now. Let's eat so that you can be my dessert," said Walter.

Tears ran down Florence's face. Florence opened her mouth and started to walk right out to confront the two of them. Twinkie grabbed Florence, put her hand over Florence's mouth and dragged her into the restroom. Wendy and I ran into the restroom right after them. Florence started crying hysterically, thinks Julie.

"You don't understand. Jenny is Jennifer Wyple: my supervisor! She's sleeping with my fiancé? What am I going to do? I got hit repeatedly in my eye so that he would be confident no one else would look at me while he could continue having an affair with my supervisor! What in the world is happening??? Walter is not on a business trip at all but at my supervisor's house. He lied to me! He's known my every move at work because he's been sleeping with my supervisor! That explains so much," said Florence.

"I'm so angry. I thought we, Walter and I could work it out. I thought we would get married. Right now, I want to confront them. But I'm feeling I shouldn't. I'm hearing that voice not to confront them. I'm listening to it this time. I don't know why. But I do want to at least see them for myself. How can I do that without letting the two of them know it's me?" asked Florence, thinks Julie.

Twinkie pulled out from her purse two huge scarves and two wigs: a long mingled gray and white haired one and a completely white haired one. Twinkie gave the long mingled gray and white haired wig to Florence. Florence put it on and wrapped one of the scarves around her head. Twinkie put on the white wig and tied her scarf around her head covering her ears. Florence adjusted her scarf to reflect the same tie on her head covering her ears as Twinkie had. Wendy removed her jacket and put it on Florence. I walked over to change shoes with her. I slipped out of my shoes and took her shoes. I was wearing my well-worn, flat black shoes.

"Rosita do you have any of your face makeup in your purse? We're gonna need it so we can darken our skin color on our faces and hands." Twinkie said.

I was glad we grabbed our purses before we left the table. I pulled out my powder brown makeup from my purse and handed it to Twinkie. Turning to Florence, Twinkie said,

"You must calm down first just until we leave out of this restaurant. You must promise me that whatever, I say or do: you will not react to Walter. We're not going that close to Walter if you do not agree. I don't want him hitting you or you letting him know you are here. Do you agree Florence?" Twinkie asked. Florence wiped her tears from her face and took a deep breath, thinks Julie.

"Yes, I agree," said Florence. Both women adjusted the wigs and large scarves over their heads. I applied the makeup to their faces and the back of their hands.

"Put your huge dark sunglasses on. Look in the mirror now," said Twinkie.

"I don't look like myself," said Florence, thinks Julie.

"Exactly, that's the point. You've got to wait until the girls come back from the table. I'm putting on my huge sunglasses too. I'm going with you to keep you focused. Watch how I walk. We can talk about what you're going to do later," said Twinkie. She turned to Wendy and me.

"Rosita, could you bring me your jacket to your suit please? Could you girls take care of the bill and we'll settle up later after we leave here please?" asked Twinkie.

"Sure," Wendy said.

Wendy and I went back to the table. We labeled and packed up all the food. We left a tip and paid the bill. I took my suit jacket to Twinkie. She put it on. It was a little too big for her but that was the purpose. When the two of them left the restroom, they were a sight. They looked like two old brown skinned ladies. Twinkie even walked a little bent over so that she appeared to be older than she was. Once Twinkie did that Florence followed Twinkie's lead with her walking. Wendy and I moved towards the front door out of the way to watch and listen, thinks Julie.

Twinkie looked like she did this before or at least she was a good actor. Linking her arm in Florence's arm, the two women walked very slowly down the isle of the east side of the restaurant to the furthest end from where Walter and Jenny were sitting. Twinkie appeared to be fussing at Florence. She changed her voice tone and said out loud,

"I told you old woman our table is on the other side." Florence followed suit. She changed her voice tone and said,

"Okay, which way to the other side old lady?"

When they completed the U-turn, they got to Walter and Jenny's table. Twinkie leaned on it for support, thinks Julie.

"Oh my old woman: look at this lovely couple. They appear to be in love," said Twinkie. Jenny smiled. Reaching in her purse, Twinkie pulled out her cell phone.

"May I take pictures of you two please? I wanna show my grands what real love looks like," said Twinkie in a trembling voice.

"Sure," said Walter. He reached over and kissed Jenny full on her lips. Twinkie snapped the picture. Next he kissed Jenny's bosom right there in the restaurant. Twinkie snapped that picture and Jenny giggled. Lastly, he wrapped his arm around Jenny's neck, pulled her close to him and the two of them just smiled towards the phone. Twinkie looked down to make sure the picture was clear. Twinkie told us later that she also felt Florence shaking right then. She snapped the last picture and pulled Florence away immediately, thinks Julie.

"Come on old woman. We got to go. Thank you so much," said Twinkie in her old ladies' trembling voice.

"That other old lady looks a little familiar. She looks a little like Florence would if she was older and darker," said Walter. Looking down at Florence's shoes, Walter said,

"We've talked so much about Florence that you got me thinking that other old woman might be Florence. Florence would never be caught in public wearing old worn black flat shoes and a mismatched jacket. You know Florence French always wears high heels when she's out and matching clothes." Julie thinks.

"Yeah she does, that's the only thing she can do I can't do for you is wear those high heels," said Jenny.

When we got Florence out of the restaurant, she began crying all over again. We got her into our parked car and saw it was parked across the street from Walter's car. I sat in the driver's seat and Twinkie sat in front on the passenger's side. Wendy sat in the back seat with Florence. Who knew that Florence only wore heels?... High heels only in public!!! I didn't but God you did, which is why you had me to switch shoes with her! Julie thinks.

Twinkie said,

"You did good, really good. You saw for yourself the two of them together. I know your heart hurts. In a situation like this, it would hurt anyone especially when it's your fiancé. Now besides wanting to do him bodily harm, what do you want to do about this Florence? We cannot make the decision for you."

"Right now I want to see for myself if Jenny gets in Walter's car and they leave together," said Florence.

"Are you sure you want to do this? Can you handle this if that's what happens? And anything else you may see?" asked Twinkie.

"Yes, I want to do this," said Florence.

"If we do this, you must not get out of the car. You must stay in the car because that is the safest place right now for you. Do you agree to stay in the car no matter what you see Florence?" asked Twinkie. Florence scrunched up her face, thinks Julie.

"No matter what I see?" asked Florence.

"No matter what you see is the agreement. Or we'll just leave now," said Twinkie. Sitting there, Florence balled up her fist, then took a deep breath and relaxed her fist. She answered Twinkie.

"I feel like I must trust whatever it is you're telling me to do. I don't like it. But I agree not to get out of the car," said Florence.

"Okay girls we're going to wait, if that's okay with you two?" asked Twinkie.

"Okay by me," said Wendy.

"It's okay with me," I said. Twinkie got out of the front seat and sat in the back with Wendy and Florence placing Florence in the middle of the back seat, thinks Julie.

We waited and watched as the two of them left the restaurant. Our car was parked almost directly across the street from Walter's car. Twinkie and Florence removed the scarves and wigs. I left the windows up, the car running and the air conditioning on. It was a very hot outside. While

Wendy and I took out our cell phones, Twinkie took out her real camera from her purse with a telescopic lens.

Right there in the middle of the afternoon, Walter and Jenny got in Walter's car together. They did not leave right away. Twinkie took pictures. We watched in shock and Florence screamed in our car. We all then understood what Walter meant when he said Jenny would be his desert. When they finally decided to leave, Walter reclined in the back seat. Jenny drove Walter's car away right before a police car drove by, thinks Julie.

Florence saw for herself. Walter and Jenny drove away together in Walter's car. We all saw everything! Tears flowed continuously down Florence's face after she stopped screaming. It was extremely sad. Twinkie had plenty of pictures.

Florence called back to work and said she wasn't feeling well. She told them she was going home for the rest of the day. She also received a text from Walter saying that his business trip was extended. He would not be home until Sunday a week later not this coming Monday as he originally stated. We drove towards Florence and Walter's condo, thinks Julie.

When Florence could finally talk, she shook her head and spoke in a trembling voice.

"This is real. It is not a dream. I pinched myself and it hurts! You were right Twinkie. And my teetee Yolanda was right! Walter only cares about himself. He never cared about me. I'm only an ornament to him. What I don't understand is why God wouldn't let me confront Walter right there in the restaurant?" asked Florence, thinks Julie.

"Well at this point, Walter does not know that you know. Nor does Jenny know you know. You also have evidence and witnesses of what's going on between the two of them. You finally have the advantage point. What are you going to do with it?" asked Twinkie.

"I don't know," said Florence. Florence remained silent the rest of the drive to her house.

We pulled up to Florence and Walter's condo building. Florence asked us to come in. We went in and sat on the couch and loveseat. Florence excused herself to their bedroom to call her teetee Yolanda. We sat in the living room whispering among ourselves, thinks Julie.

"You know it's time for her to leave," I whispered to Twinkie and Wendy.

"Yeah, I know but it has to be her decision. We cannot suggest nor make this decision for her. If we do, she will blame us when she does not have Walter. It's her choice ladies," whispered Twinkie.

"I agree. That's what I'm feeling in my spirit and definitely what God is saying," whispered Wendy.

"Okay, I won't say anything," I whispered, thinks Julie.

Florence returned from her bedroom with a distraught look on her face.

"My teetee Yolanda can't talk right now. She's at work in the middle of something. She'll call me the first chance she gets. Guys I really don't know what to do. Do you have any suggestions? What do you think I should do? Or could you just tell me what to do please?" asked Florence.

Florence started crying all over again and sunk into the loveseat next to me. Twinkie, Wendy and I looked at each other. I wrapped my arm around her shoulders letting her cry leaning on my chest. I couldn't say a word. God you wouldn't let me. Wendy started to come over when Florence's cell phone rang. She pulled it from her pocket and said it was her aunt. Florence excused herself and talked with her aunt in her bedroom, thinks Julie.

While Florence was in her bedroom, Twinkie talked very low. Twinkie said we must pray for Florence to see clearly and that God reveals the consequences of which ever decision Florence makes right now in Jesus name. We all agreed in prayer right before Florence returned to the living room.

When Florence returned she was a little calmer at first. Then she started shaking as she sat down. Florence told us her aunt wouldn't tell her what to do either. Her teetee Yolanda only prayed with Florence for her to make the right decision. Her aunt explained to Florence that we were not allowed to make the decision for Florence. Wow! God you gave immediate confirmation we were doing the right thing! Julie thinks.

Florence also told us her aunt was leaving work and coming straight to the condo. Florence held her head. She said she was tired and so sleepy. Twinkie told her perhaps she should take a nap. Then Twinkie asked Florence what was Walter's number? So in case, her cell phone rang, we would know not to wake her up until she was ready to talk. Florence was so tired and sleepy that she did not realize what Twinkie was doing. When Florence called out Walter's cell number, we all put it in our cell phones so that we would know if he tried to call any of us at a later time.

Twinkie said we would stay until her aunt got there. Florence thanked us, left her cell phone on the living room table and went to bed. We got our food from the car and ate it. We put Florence's food in the refrigerator. Her aunt arrived about an hour and a half later. We let her in, talked with her and showed her some of the pictures, thinks Julie.

Huh, her teetee Yolanda is something else! She told us to let Florence sleep so that you: God could work on Florence's mind and speak to Florence in her sleep. TeeTee Yolanda said a little sleep and a lot of God helps us all. She also said God knew this was going to happen. It was no surprise to you God. You know God: TeeTee Yolanda was right. You knew all along what was going on between Walter and Jenny: Florence's supervisor. Wow! You saw it all God.

TeeTee Yolanda took all our numbers and she gave us her cell number. We also forwarded a few choice pictures to her cell phone for evidence. We realized Florence never took a picture because she was so distraught, which was totally understandable. Then TeeTee Yolanda told us to go home or wherever we were going. She suggested that we get some rest because you: God was going to make it very clear to Florence what the consequences would be with whatever decision Florence made. That was a confirmation for the three of us of what we prayed before TeeTee Yolanda came, thinks Julie.

TeeTee Yolanda asked us to stay prayerful. This was her specialty and gift since she experienced this with her first husband. She volunteered and worked in women's shelters. TeeTee Yolanda pointed out that there was an entire weekend and a week to make whatever changes necessary, so be available for whichever way God worked it out.

TeeTee Yolanda said Florence's family was on standby waiting to assist in the matter. They just wanted it to be Florence's decision. Her sister, Florence's mom was not very rational when it came to anyone hurting her baby. Thus, Florence's dad was keeping Florence's mom occupied and TeeTee Yolanda was the calmest person to be around Florence right then. She prayed with us and kicked us out, thinks Julie.

Driving home we discussed the events of the day. We thanked you God that Florence was alive! We thanked you God that there was time for Florence to leave with no trace should she decide to. We thanked you God that Florence had her family's support. We also thanked you God that neither Walter nor Jenny was aware Florence knew about their relationship.

We praised you God, then TeeTee Yolanda texted us. She told us to check and see if there was a dark blue car following us? Twinkie and Wendy both looked out the back window and it was! Wendy texted back to her "yes!" TeeTee Yolanda texted us again: "Whatever we do, DO NOT GO HOME! Call 911 and go to a police station instead." Julie thinks.

TeeTee Yolanda texted that car followed us from when we left Florence's condo building. She texted it was the same car that followed her to work earlier in the week when she left Florence's condo. TeeTee Yolanda texted that the car pulled off right after we left and a green car pulled up in its place. The person in the green car used binoculars to watch Florence's condo and TeeTee Yolanda closed the blinds.

She texted us more instructions: Do not call Florence until TeeTee Yolanda said it was okay! She texted she was assessing how much stuff Florence had to move when she found a running tape recorder. The tape recorder was hidden in a closet with wires hooked up throughout the condo. TeeTee Yolanda immediately texted her husband: Johnny, a Chicago police detective. He was on his way right then. TeeTee Yolanda texted she was glad Florence was still asleep, thinks Julie.

Wendy called 911 and gave them the license plate number of the car following us.

"Where is the nearest police station to turn into from where we are?" asked Wendy.

The 911 operator gave us exact instructions on what to do. We were told to stop two blocks before the police station. A black unmarked squad car was on that same block. We were to pull up across the street from the black squad car and park as if we were going to a house there. They wanted to make sure the blue car was following us. We all started praying, thinks Julie.

When we did, the blue car pulled up right behind us and parked. We were told if that happened, we were to wait a few minutes, start up our car again and then drive into the police station parking lot two blocks away. The black squad car would handle things from there. That blue car followed us and slowed down when we pulled into the police station. Once we were parked in the police parking lot, the blue car drove away. The black squad car followed the blue car into the next block and pulled the blue car over.

An officer met us in the parking lot. We told him we were the ones, who called 911. We had come from a friend's condo building when we noticed a car following us. We didn't know why. We definitely didn't want it following us home. We didn't know the person or whose car it was, thinks Julie.

We watched down the block to see what would happen. The blue car left and black squad car came to us in the police parking lot. The officer said the man, who followed us was private investigator from We See it All Agency. He was hired by a Walter Harris! His instructions were to follow anyone, who came to the condo complex with Florence French. The man had a picture of this Florence French, a camera with a telescopic lens, video equipment and a tape recorder. He said Harris paid him in advance to watch his fiancée while he was away.

He said this was not the first time. He followed Harris' fiancée many times before whenever Harris was out of town. She only went to the store, to the gym, to her parents' house, to the shopping mall and back-and-forth to work. Harris told him not to follow Florence French this time just to follow whoever came to the condo with her and left. That's why he was following you ladies. He showed us his private investigator's license so we had to let him go, thinks Julie.

We thanked the officers and left. While we drove, you God gave us insight. Twinkie explained the reason why Florence couldn't make a decision was because of the blinders and scales on her eyes spiritually. Twinkie told us we must agree in prayer that the deception did not continue. That the blinders and scales be removed from Florence's eyes. We prayed just that and requested the removal of all generational curses. We stopped to develop the film from Twinkie's camera and we printed out all the pictures from our cell phones.

We picked up something to eat and took it home. Wendy and I still had to go to work the next day. We talked for a while. But after all the excitement and battle, we realized we were tired ourselves. We each talked with our own guy and apprised him of the situation. Twinkie spent the night with us. I changed my linen and gave Twinkie my bedroom. I slept on the couch, thinks Julie.

Early the following morning after we had all finished our individual prayers alone with you God, we gathered in the living room. We were talking and sitting on the couch and loveseat before Wendy and I prepared for work. We all received a text from TeeTee Yolanda with an update.

Florence wasn't going to work. She called off sick. She woke up in hysterics. God gave Florence choices in her dreams and showed Florence the consequences of her decisions. As a matter of fact, Florence had three dreams that night. Her uncles Johnny and Daniel talked with Florence so she could calm down. Florence talked and prayed with all of them: her uncles and her teetee Yolanda. No one told Florence what to do. Everyone just gave her the facts. Florence made a decision that the entire family was working on, thinks Julie.

Next, Florence texted us and said she was moving out. She asked us to help her pack after work. Twinkie texted her and told her she was still in town. Twinkie could come and help while Wendy and I were at work. Florence texted and said she would give Twinkie a call after she filed an order of protection at the local court building against Walter. Florence texted she wasn't sure if she had to go to a local court building or downtown to the Daly Center.

TeeTee Yolanda called us to give us an update while Florence was in the shower and dressing in the other room. We put her on speaker so we all could hear. (I was glad I had already gotten my shower. I know Wendy was glad she had gotten her shower early too.) Uncles Johnny and Daniel spent the night with the women. They were sleeping now. They listened to all Walter had recorded. Walter had left the tape recorder running when he beat up

Florence on that Tuesday and left the condo. Uncles Johnny and Daniel turned the tape recorder off, disconnected it and took that tape for evidence. They heard our conversations as well. Uncles Johnny and Daniel found all the hidden microphones in the condo with a remote transmitter to turn it on and turn it off. They also disconnected that, thinks Julie.

Uncle Johnny had the police in the area check out the person parked in the green car that was still there when he arrived. That man was another private investigator from We See it All Agency. He was waiting for Florence to leave and follow whoever left with Florence. The police told him to leave or they would take him in as they had received a complaint of a "peeping Tom" watching women from a green car. The investigator left with no problem.

I had wondered what Walter meant when he said he made sure Florence was taken care of. I thought it was the fact Walter beat her up. No it was both! He beat her and Walter had someone watching her every move! He does not trust her at all. What would Walter have done to Florence if she was cheating on him like he is cheating on her? Walter Harris is something else and very dangerous as Twinkie had warned, thinks Julie.

Right before Wendy and I walked out the door to work (we had planned to go in early to work to see if we could get off early), Florence called Twinkie. Twinkie put Florence on her cell phone speaker. Florence changed her mind and asked Twinkie, if she could come right away? Florence explained she felt very uncomfortable staying in the condo after talking with her uncles Johnny and Daniel. What they shared shook her up and what God revealed in two of the dreams scared Florence into reality. She said she could see clearly now. Florence admitted that if she stayed, she would be dead! That was one of the dreams. She had decided to live and not die.

Florence said she decided to cooperate with God. God had something better for her, which was her third dream. Florence said she just had to get her mind right and prepared to receive it. Florence said what God showed her in that third dream was the second time she dreamed it. It was something she dreamed of in high school, thinks Julie.

Twinkie told Florence she was on her way and hung up with Florence. Wendy and I grabbed clothes to change into after work. Twinkie admonished us to watch and see if anyone was following us at all. She said the private investigator may not have told the officers the complete truth. She warned us to call the police or get an order of protection ourselves if we suspected or thought we saw Walter Harris. I gave Twinkie our spare keys to lock up after she left. We agreed to keep each other posted and prayed. Wendy and I left for work.

Twinkie told us later that she was glad to be on the other end and not to be the victim. Although she felt the pressure, Twinkie said it was totally different being able to help. She told us that she and TeeTee Yolanda went with Florence to her Human Resource Department to discuss Florence's situation. Florence requested a leave of absence for three months effective immediately to protect her life. Florence put in paperwork to transfer to the Lake County office upon her return. And no one, especially not her immediate supervisor, was to know where she had been transferred to! Julie thinks.

Florence went to the bank and removed all her

money from her and Walter's joint account. She closed her separate account too. Florence opened up an account in the bank across the street. After placing all her money there, she had all her bank mail sent to her teetee Yolanda's house. Next she went to her credit union. She gave them her teetee Yolanda's address for regular mail delivery from the credit union.

When we got there in the evening, Florence's mom and her other family members had almost completely packed everything. They left all of Walter's things and the tape recorder sitting in the middle of the floor. Florence's mom was really upset and watched from the window to see if anyone was watching her daughter's condo. As soon as she saw the telescopic lens, she recorded the license plate number of the car and stepped away from the blinds. Then Florence's mom called the police to say there was a "peeping Tom" watching her window. After the police came and the man left, they immediately moved everything of Florence's out of the building. Julie thinks.

We all discovered over the next few weeks that Walter Harris had all our cell phone numbers! Because once he discovered Florence was gone, he tried to contact each of us. We realized Walter must have gone through Florence's purse our reunion night after she went to sleep and entered our cell numbers into his cell phone. Not only did we have to block Walter's number but we each had to go to a court house and get an order of protection against him.

Wow! That was some experience. We participated in a domestic violence situation as peers. Florence is fine today. She's in counseling and is still alive! I received a text from her the other day with her new cell phone number. Since all the bills were in Walter's name, Florence had money! She was never broke and had enough to get a new place near her new job location. Florence just needed Jesus to help her get her life straight. I'm so glad God you helped! Florence is going to be okay. She's getting ready for her dreams to come true by you God, thinks Julie.

I didn't understand all that was involved when it happened to Mama. Yet, I'm very grateful Mama did leave Daddy. If she had not, she might not be alive today. And Mama finally did meet someone else at her church. He may become my stepdad and that's okay with me. Mama lights up whenever she talks about him. Mama said she dreamed of a man, who would treat her as Christ loves the church and so far, this man has a great tract record.

I took the time to look him up in the criminal and civil systems myself. I also investigated his business. He owns his own business and has his own cars. That's right God, this man has his own "plural" cars! I'm so excited. But nothing surprises you. You knew that already. I'm surprised it took my pretty mama so long to decide she was ready for someone else. God: you are something else yourself! You're fulfilling Mama's dreams, Wendy's dreams, Percy's dreams, Florence's dreams, and Jerred's dreams, thinks Julie.

Now there are my dreams. I remember when you let me see an old friend change to a new friend or should I say change to a mature friend in one of my dreams (at least that's the interpretation I received from you). I could not quite see the face until... Just then Julie's watch rings and jolts her out of her thoughts.

Julie gets up to shower. After her shower, she puts on fresh clean matching blue undergarments and her black full length slip. She goes to her bedroom. Shuffling through the stockings in her drawer she locates a black pair. I'm wearing my black fishnet stockings with this dress, thinks Julie.

While dressing, thoughts about what tonight maybe like with Jerred flood her head. Will we talk most of the night, I wonder? I love talking with Jerred, Jesus. Jerred can talk as much as I can. I also like the fact that Jerred listens to you, Jesus and loves to pray. Will Jerred think of something new to pray about tonight? Julie thinks.

Hearing the front door open, Julie asks loudly,

"Wen is that you?"

"Yeah, it's me. We had a surprised late meeting today. How are you doing? How was your day?" asks Wendy.

"It was okay. I'll be out in a minute to talk about it and get your opinion on my dress. I'm going out with Jerred tonight," says Julie.

"Okay give me a few minutes. I have to go to the restroom after being in traffic. I'll talk with you then," says Wendy.

Continuing in her thoughts, Julie thinks about her friends. I know I never told Wendy my high school secret about Jerred. I always desired a male friend in high school that I could talk to about other things and about you: Jesus. Jerred told me he received you: Jesus in his heart when we were sophomores. I remember telling you Jesus how I like Jerred but he played around too much. He was rarely serious, thinks Julie.

Yet, when I watched how Jerred interacted with our classmates, I realized Jerred possessed integrity, a great character and a good temperament when he wasn't joking around. So I asked you God for a friend like Jerred without all those jokes to be my friend because I saw how Jerred was a good friend to other people like Twinkie, Percy, Earl and Florence.

I watched how he respected his mother, whenever she came to our school. I asked you in high school if I could have a husband, who would be my best friend like Jerred and still love You? Over the years, Jerred has learned to balance his comical side with his serious side and his spiritual side. I found out laughter is good for our souls. And these days, I find myself laughing at Jerred's jokes, Julie thinks as she smiles.

Besides you, Jesus, Wendy's my best friend and has been all these years. Jerred is my new best friend. We talk about a lot of things and we pray together almost nightly. Now I'll have two human best friends that are totally unique. Both of my best friends are fun to be around.

There is a difference in having a man as a best friend. I realize you God are answering my secret prayers and fulfilling my dreams. You are giving me as your Word says: *"... the desires of thine heart (Psalm 37:4b KJV)...* of my heart."

I guess I could finally share my high school secret with Wendy. What are friends for if you can't share your secrets with them? Isn't that what has been happening all these years since I was little? Huh, isn't that how Wendy and I stayed such good friends? Wendy shared her high school secret because I'm her friend. She's my friend and I have a secret, thinks Julie.

After spraying on her favorite cologne on certain parts of her body, Julie exits her bedroom into their living room. She sits on their couch waiting for Wendy to show up and critique her evening outfit. Wendy walks into their living room wrapping her robe around herself and sits on the loveseat across from Julie. Julie stands and twirls around to show off her outfit for her date with Jerred.

"You look great! I like that color on you. I'm surprised though that you aren't wearing red," says Wendy.

"Thanks for the compliment. Yeah, I know it's not red but this blue is Jerred's favorite color," says Julie.

"Well you look good. Have fun on your date with Jerred. Percy is working late tonight so I'm going to rest for now and talk with him later," says Wendy.

"Before Jerred gets here, I have something to tell you. As my friend, I feel I can tell you. Did I ever tell you my high school dreams and my high school secret?" asks Julie.

Well God, here I go again sharing my secret with my friend, thinks Julie.

About the Author

P. Lee May enjoys sharing and telling stories to her family and friends. She has four children and six grandchildren with more to come. She possesses a dual Bachelor of Arts degree in Organizational Communications and English Writing from North Central College in Naperville, IL.

She realizes that friends are valuable, especially those you can confide in and trust with your secrets. These friends possess integrity because you can count on them not to embarrass you or reveal your personal business. Real friends are few in number and hard to find.

Ms. May shares a message of encouragement, hope, and laughter wherever she goes. Ms. May loves to see you smile. What greater smile can a person have than one where they enjoy what they read?

This is the first of many teenage and young adult books to come. She writes and creates skits, plays, books, mini books, and workbooks.

She travels around the world and has been to places like Kobe, Japan; Osaka, Japan; Memphis, TN; Orlando, FL; Milwaukee, WI; Niagara Falls, NY; Picayune, MS; Dallas, TX; Tylertown, MS; Maui, HI; and Ciudad Guzman, Jalisco, Mexico.

Her other books are:

Parent focused books

- Protecting Your Child in Prayer
- You're Gonna Make it! ... A Christian guide of wisdom keys for single parents

Children's book:

- Laurie's Secret

Spiritual warfare books
- Since Jesus Came into My House
- Taking Authority Over Your Neighborhood

Ms. May is available for seminars and meetings.